Enjoy the Little Things

Enjoy the Little Things

Karen Ramsey

One

I lie down on McKenzie's unmade bed, my muscles numb from exhaustion. McKenzie is at her desk, long brown ringlets cascading over her shoulders as she hunches over her laptop. A USB cord trails from the computer to her camera.

"I can't seem to get the saturation right," she mutters. Though I can't see her face, I know her forehead is scrunched up, her lips pursed in concentration.

Curiosity gets the best of me. Bouncing up from the bed, I peer over her shoulder. On the screen is an image of a car accident. Shards of glass sparkle like glitter on the asphalt. A blue Honda Civic is wedged up on the sidewalk, the back hugging the traffic light pole. The driver-side door is no longer attached. If you could even call it a door anymore. The hunk of metal is lying on the ground, bent into a half-moon shape.

Inside the car, the airbags are blown out and deployed. A tiny box from the photo editor highlights the front of the airbag. McKenzie hits a couple of keys and huffs in frustration.

"What are you trying to do?" I ask.

"I'm trying to make the red pop."

I stare at the picture, seeing nothing but a white, chalky airbag. I open my mouth to point this out when a deep red seeps into the airbag.

"Ah, that's better."

I glance at her, surprised. Why is she editing a photo like this?

She turns to me, smiling in satisfaction. "So, how was dance rehearsal?" A deep gash has appeared on her forehead, and blood streams down the right side of her face.

I wake with a start. Clutching a hand over my racing heart, I gasp for breath.

It all comes rushing back to me. The accident happened on Memorial Day. The Williams were having their annual pool party, and McKenzie was headed over early to spend time with her boyfriend, Justin, and help set up. I should have been with her, but I got stuck at home babysitting my little sister Shelby. The minute my dad walked through the door, I grabbed my keys and bolted. I was only an hour behind McKenzie.

"Be careful," my dad called out. "There are a lot of crazies out today."

"Got it. Love you!" I shouted as the door swung closed behind me.

Red and blue flashing lights flooded my vision as I pulled up to a red light. I glanced over, surveying the scene. A few police cars occupied the curb, but I didn't see any wounded passengers or signs of an ambulance. Upon closer inspection, a glint of metal caught my eye—a small silver chain dangling from the rearview mirror. Then it dawned on me.

I knew the car—McKenzie's blue Honda Civic.

I immediately pulled over, a palo verde tree providing little shade against the blazing Arizona sun. My flip-flops thwacked the pavement as I rushed to the scene.

The whole time, my eyes were trained on McKenzie's car. From somewhere in the distance, an officer was yelling at someone to stay away. It took the officer placing his hand on my shoulder for me to realize he was shouting at me.

"What happened?" I asked, breathless.

"Ma'am, I'm sorry. I can't release that information. I need you to return to your vehicle."

"No!" I cried. "I need to know what happened to the girl in the Honda." I pointed at the car.

The officer's face remained stern. "You need to return to your vehicle."

Frustrated, I raced back to my car. As I opened the driver-side door, already paging through my phone contacts, the caller ID popped up, showing a call from MOM2. I answered, caught off guard when I heard the voice of Mr. Foster, McKenzie's dad. He told me she had been in an accident and informed me which hospital they had gone to. After hanging up, I tried to start my car with a trembling hand.

When I first arrived at the hospital, McKenzie was in surgery. I met Mr. and Mrs. Foster in the waiting room. Several hours later, we were escorted to the intensive care unit. I knew that McKenzie being in the ICU meant the injuries were significant. The hospital floor was eerily quiet. The nurse led us to McKenzie's room, and I drew a deep breath before entering.

More tubes than I could count fed into McKenzie's nose, mouth, and body, and a quiet beeping filled the silence. There was a brace on her left arm, an IV drip in her right hand. Her face was bruised, her left eye swollen shut. My eyes were drawn to a huge gash on her forehead that had been stitched shut. The rest of her was hidden under the covers. All the images my mind had conjured up on the drive over didn't compare to what lay before me. My imagination had been much more forgiving.

Mrs. Foster gasped, and sobs began racking her body. Mr. Foster wrapped her in his arms, his eyes filling with tears. I just stood there, staring at my friend. *She's broken, but she could recover.*

The first night in the hospital, I found a small chapel on the first floor. All the pews faced a wooden cross at the pulpit. To the right, there was an altar to light candles. The pew creaked when I sat. On my first visit, I didn't say much. It was just a quiet place to fall apart. But as days turned into a week and the prognosis didn't improve, I started to pray, to beg. "God, please heal her. She's my best friend, you know? I can't live without her, and she's all the Fosters have. Please, for them, for me… Please wake her up."

Each time, I hoped I'd walk into her room and she'd be awake, or the nurse would rush in and report there had been some unexplainable progress—she took a turn for the better, would make a full recovery. No such report came. Instead, the doctor walked in and explained that McKenzie had suffered significant internal injuries along with a traumatic brain injury. After monitoring her brain activity for the last few days, they saw no improvement. At this point, it was not likely McKenzie would ever wake up. It was up to the Fosters to decide what the next steps would be.

I stormed out of the room and marched to the chapel. As usual, it was empty. I stood in the middle of the aisle, glaring at the cross. "What are you thinking?" I hissed. "She's my best friend! She is everything to me. So, you better fix this. If you take her from me, we're through. Do you hear me? *Through!*" As hot tears rolled down my cheeks, I collapsed to the floor and wept.

When I returned to McKenzie's room, there was a heaviness that hadn't been there before. Mrs. Foster told me they'd made the decision to turn off life support. My body went numb. They couldn't turn off the machines. I needed her. The world needed her. She *had* to live. But twenty-four hours later, the machines were unplugged, and McKenzie slipped away peacefully.

I wish my imagination would be forgiving now. It's been a week since McKenzie died, and the nightmares are relentless. I stare at my ceiling and watch the fan blades spin. Sunlight pours in through a crack in my window curtains.

I grab my phone and will myself to click on my photo gallery. Mrs. Foster called a few days ago and asked if I would be interested in speaking at the funeral. She also asked if I have any photos of McKenzie for a slideshow. To be honest, I don't have many pictures; McKenzie was the photographer.

I know one of the first pictures will show my sister Shelby in the kitchen covered in flour. McKenzie had been there when it was taken, trying to regain composure after watching flour explode all over Shelby. The picture is fuzzy because I was laughing too. My thumb presses the album and there Shelby is. If I swipe right, McKenzie's face will eventually be there too. I suck in a deep breath and swipe the screen.

The next photo is McKenzie, long brunette ringlets falling over her shoulders. Her arms are wrapped around Shelby, whose sandy blonde hair is tied in pigtails. McKenzie is resting her chin on Shelby's shoulder, both of them looking directly into the lens, huge smiles plastered on their faces. It's definitely a picture worth sharing. Not just because it's a good shot, but because it clearly shows the bond McKenzie and Shelby shared. The next photo displays the ingredients for the sugar cookies we were baking that day. My eyes fill with tears.

When footsteps sound in the hallway, I quickly wipe my eyes. Shelby shuffles into my room and sits next to me. The ingredients are still pulled up on my phone.

"That was a fun day," Shelby comments after peering at the photo. I nod.

She sighs. "I really miss Tenzie."

The nickname brings back sweet memories. I was always calling McKenzie "Kenzie." At age four, Shelby was unable to pronounce *K* sounds, so any time Shelby said her name, it came out "Tenzie." The nickname stuck, even four years later.

I glance over as tears fill Shelby's eyes. "I didn't get to say goodbye."

I reach over and pull her in, her tears soaking my shirt.

"She misses you too," I say, my voice breaking.

I swallow, trying not to cry. My parents didn't think Shelby was ready, so they had decided to keep her home when McKenzie was in the hospital. Plus, the ICU didn't allow children under the age of twelve, so she wouldn't have been able to come anyway. I knew that would be hard for her. McKenzie was her other big sister—she was always here.

I let Shelby cry as I hold her tight. Seeing her hurting makes my heart ache even more. Once she gains her composure, I wipe the remaining tears from her face.

"Do you want to help me?" I ask.

"With what?" She stares up at me with her big blue eyes.

"Well, the Fosters want pictures of Tenzie to share. I thought you could help me pick some out."

"Yeah." She smiles up at me.

I open my phone to the photo of ingredients and scroll to the right. McKenzie's smiling face, her arms around Shelby, fills the screen. I inhale deeply to keep myself together. Shelby grabs my hand.

"I love this picture," she says.

"Me too," I whisper, squeezing Shelby's hand. "Let's see what else we have." I find a selfie of McKenzie sticking out her tongue. She had snapped it during lunch one day and set it as my screensaver without telling me. When I checked my phone later during class, I started chuckling. A few students looked at me, and I quickly slid my phone in my bag and got back to work. The picture remained my screensaver until Shelby had her ballet recital and I switched it to her wearing an adorable pink tutu and ballet flats.

I swipe, and there is a picture of me and McKenzie with Shelby sandwiched in between us outside the auditorium. Shelby is holding the small bouquet of flowers McKenzie had brought her. McKenzie had made a sarcastic remark about all the Lanter girls being born to dance. Shelby had glanced over at me with a huge grin on her face. She was so proud to take after her older sister.

"Wait, go back," Shelby pipes up.

I return to the picture of McKenzie's funny face. A small giggle escapes Shelby's lips. "She always makes funny faces," she says. I grin, remembering how McKenzie could change your sour mood with a goofy face. Shelby and I continue to lounge upstairs until we're called to dinner. Together, we select about fifteen pictures of McKenzie.

Shelby and I are heading downstairs when I ask her, "Hey, do you want to say goodbye to Tenzie?"

Shelby nods emphatically. "How?"

"I'm giving a speech at Tenzie's funeral. You could write something."

Shelby hesitates. "I don't want to talk in front of everyone."

"That's okay. I'll read it for you."

"Well…maybe I can write something."

I email the pictures to Delia after dinner and hope I sent them in time to use at the funeral. I then take out a notebook and flip it to a blank page. I stare, tapping my pen on the empty page. I start my speech several times, and each time the page is torn out and crumpled in the trash can. Fresh tears trail down my cheeks. How am I supposed to say goodbye to my best friend, my partner in crime?

I pause, grab my phone, and pull up my voicemail. I hit play on the last message McKenzie left me and inspiration strikes.

The funeral is held at our church the week after McKenzie's passing. Staring in the mirror, I know that no amount of concealer is going to hide the dark circles under my steel-blue eyes. I don't even know why I've bothered to wear makeup. It will most likely be wiped away by the time the funeral is over. I run a finger through my ash blonde hair to loosen the curls, creating soft waves. I look down at my knee-length black dress with a faux wrap style. It's the same one I wore to my great-grandmother's funeral just last year. I was sad when my great-grandma passed, but she had lived out East. We only visited a couple of times. I didn't really know her. But this is different. McKenzie was my best friend, and we knew everything about each other. I feel like half of my heart has been ripped away.

I pull into the parking lot an hour early, hiding in one of the back rooms until the service is about to start. I didn't want to listen to all the clichés, like "time heals all wounds" or "she's in a better place." How is time going to heal this gaping hole in my chest? A hole that formed when my best friend was taken from the only place she should be—here.

I wait until it's quiet in the lobby before I wander toward the sanctuary. The room is packed. It seems like our entire youth group is here, along with family and friends. The Fosters are up front, along with Nana and Papa Foster and Grandma and Grandpa Madden, Mrs. Foster's parents. I try to focus anywhere but the stage. There, McKenzie's closed casket rests beside a flower wreath and her senior photo. I sit next to Mrs. Foster. She takes my hand and squeezes it tight, not taking her eyes off the smiling photo.

Though I agreed to speak, my stomach starts to knot. I'm not sure if I can go through with this. When the pastor locks eyes with me, I draw a calming breath and step up to the podium, opening my speech.

"Sexy, gorgeous, hot stuff, lovely, Kels, K—on any given day, these are the greetings I would receive in person or over the phone." My voice catches, and I pause. "McKenzie always knew how to light up someone's day. She just had this way about her. I loved to be near her. From the beginning, McKenzie was determined to be my friend. She forced me to talk to her, and let me tell you, this girl was relentless. Once we became friends, she dragged me everywhere. She hated sitting. She never wanted to miss anything, even the little things.

"I think that's why McKenzie loved photography. To capture the moment and never forget it. She took pictures of everything, and I do mean *every*thing." I hear a few chuckles from the crowd. When I look up, several heads nod in agreement. I catch sight of Justin, sitting alone in the back with a grin on his face. "I know the world was better with her. She touched the lives of so many. She will be deeply missed."

I pause, setting my speech aside and pulling out Shelby's. The little note telling me not to read it until today stares up at me. "I wasn't the only member of my household who was attached to McKenzie. Those who have been around a while know Shelby is my sister, but because the three of us were always together, many thought we were all related. Shelby wanted to share something as well." I clear my throat. "Tenzie"—I smile and quickly explain the name—"had curly hair. I wish I had her hair sometimes. But more than that now, I really wish she'd walk through my door again."

Tears blur the words on the page, and the whole room grows quiet, patiently waiting for me to continue. I hear the creak of a chair, and then footsteps on the stairs. Suddenly, there is a small hand grabbing mine. I don't even hesitate to bend down and give Shelby a hug. I don't care that a room full of people are watching, waiting for me to finish. I take a second before standing again, Shelby still holding my hand.

I continue. "Sometimes, Tenzie would come over just to see me. She said she liked spending time with me. We would play with dolls, or play hairdresser. I really miss her. I want her to come back. People have said I will see her again. I hope so. I love you, Tenzie." When I finish, I gather the speeches and lead Shelby back to my seat. She crawls into my lap and leans her head on my shoulder. Delia, McKenzie's mom, reaches over and takes her hand. Shelby motions that she wants to sit in her lap, and when Delia nods, Shelby moves over and wraps her arms around Delia's neck.

The pastor takes the stage once more, speaking for the remainder of the funeral service. Before the service concludes, volunteers present the slideshow. It starts with pictures of McKenzie as a little girl. Next, we see shots of her and me in elementary school, and her with her parents. It concludes with several pictures Shelby and I had picked out, plus a few Justin must have chosen. But when I peek back, Justin has already left the room.

Getting through the burial takes every ounce of strength I have left. The pain constricting my heart is excruciating, my chest tightening until my breathing comes ragged. After everyone leaves, I continue to stand there, just staring at the hole in the ground. If I leave, it makes it final. And I don't want it to be final. Eventually, I meander back to my car.

I tried so hard not to cry in front of the Fosters. For the most part, I was successful. But now that I'm finally alone in my car, I break down in tears. I grasp the steering wheel with a white-knuckle grip. I never knew it was possible to feel this much pain. For a moment, I don't think I'll be able to survive this.

I just spent the morning listening to the pastor drone on about how even in death, God is good. Well, I don't believe God is good anymore. In fact, I want to scream at God for doing this, for taking my best friend. But yelling at Him means acknowledging His existence, and at this moment, I don't know if He is really out there.

Because if God existed, I wouldn't be at a cemetery right now.

At the luncheon held inside the church, several people stop me to give their condolences, including the girls from the youth group. After chatting for a minute, I politely excuse myself. Scanning the room, I realize I haven't seen Justin since the burial. Maybe he went home.

When I step outside to get some air and escape the crowd, I notice the side door to the youth room propped open. I walk over and let myself in, struck by the sound of sobbing. I'm not sure if I should stay, so I turn to walk out.

"Kelsey?" Justin asks. His eyes are rimmed with red.

"Hey," I whisper. "Sorry to walk in."

"It's okay," he mumbles. Then, silence.

"I'll leave." I take a step toward the door.

"You don't have to. You can stay," he says. I wander into the room of folding chairs and sit next to him.

Digging through my purse, I pull out a tube of lipstick. "I thought you might want this," I say, handing it to him. He takes the lipstick, sliding the lid off and twisting it up. He gazes at it, a faint smile tugging at the corners of his mouth.

During freshman year, Sarah Greenwald hosted a co-ed birthday party. I was hesitant about going, but McKenzie promised we would have a blast. On the way out, she grabbed her red lipstick, which she rarely wore.

"Really?" I raised my eyebrows.

"You never know. It might come in handy."

At the party, one of the girls suggested we all play seven minutes in heaven. Everyone wrote their names down on scraps of paper. The boys' names were put into one bucket, and the girls' into another. When a name was drawn from each bucket, those two had to go into the closet for seven minutes. The first two people drawn were our classmates Mike and Emily. There was a chorus of *ooh*s as they closed the door. Someone set the timer, and a hush swept over the room as we all tried to hear what was going on in the closet. When the timer buzzed, Sarah knocked on the door. No one answered. She opened it to find Mike and Emily lip-locked. A couple of the guys whistled, and the two tore away from each other. Emily's cheeks burned bright red, but Mike simply bowed.

Justin and McKenzie's names were picked next. Justin was new to the area, though we had seen him around school and at church a few times. Justin motioned for McKenzie to enter the closet first, then followed her in. The room again went quiet. When the seven minutes were up, McKenzie stumbled out laughing, fresh red lipstick coloring her lips. Justin walked out with smudged lipstick around his mouth and a lip print on his cheek. When McKenzie saw me gawking at them, she winked. I noticed Justin glance back at her and smile, blushing slightly.

I got the whole story later that night at McKenzie's house as we sat in her room eating Oreos. Once the closet door had shut, they had just…talked. He told her how his family had moved from Houston, Texas since his dad accepted the new youth pastor role for our church. He'd met Sarah at school, and that's how he wound up at her party. Right before the seven minutes were up, they'd decided to make it look like they'd done something. She pulled out her red lipstick, and he smeared it on his lips. Then she politely asked if she could kiss his cheek. When he said yes, she applied her lipstick and kissed him. I could tell she had a crush on him, and from the smile on his face after he'd walked out of the closet, he felt the same. McKenzie wore red lipstick to every party after that, especially to parties at Justin's house. It was their inside joke.

That much is apparent by the way he now caps the tube and clutches it tight.

"Thanks." Justin's voice breaks on the word. "You did good today," he adds. "You looked a little surprised when you read Shelby's speech."

"I was. She told me not to read it beforehand. I honestly didn't know McKenzie used to come over just to hang out with her."

"That was McKenzie, making everyone feel special."

"Always." I smile.

He stands, sticking the tube of lipstick in his pocket as he ambles to the door. "Do you need the room?"

"Nah. Just came in because I saw the door open," I say, nodding at the door.

"Yeah, I guess I just needed space. A little time to pray, ya know?"

"Not really. Him and I aren't really speaking," I growl.

"I get that," he says, but his face falls. "It's not His fault, though."

I want to argue, but I bite my tongue. Of course this is His fault. The only reason I'm sitting in a sanctuary right now is to say goodbye. After this, I don't plan on stepping into a church again. Ever.

Two

It's been six weeks since the funeral, and I've been adamant about not attending church despite my mom's constant nudging.

"But Kelsey isn't going," Shelby whines from the hallway.

"Shelby, I'm not arguing with you. Shoes, now!" my dad yells.

Two weeks ago, I overheard Shelby complaining that she shouldn't have to go to church if I didn't have to. I didn't hear my mom's explanation, but it was enough to appease my eight-year-old sister at the time. Now, she stomps down the hallway.

Once my family leaves, I stare at the boxes stacked in the corner of my room. In a couple of weeks, all these boxes will be packed into my car, and I'll be off to college. When I graduated, I was ecstatic. College meant freedom, adulthood. McKenzie and I would be attending the same university, and even though we didn't have our dorm assignment yet, we hoped we would be together. I glance at my computer, thinking of all the unopened emails about my dorm assignment, my schedule, all the first-day need-to-knows, et cetera. I only skimmed through one letter for the move-in date, letting everything else just rot in my inbox. I'm too afraid to check the roommate list. My heart can't take any more damage, and if I see that McKenzie was supposed to be my roommate, it might crumble completely.

I ignore my computer and my unfinished packing, and instead get ready for work.

Before the accident, I was a model employee. I smiled at the customers, carried on a conversation, sympathized with them about the high prices, and apologized for things completely out of my control. Now, I can't bring myself to care. Missing out on twenty-five cents won't kill anyone. During today's shift, a customer catches me rolling my eyes and complains to Mr. Avery, my manager. He pulls me into his office.

"Kelsey, I know you've had a rough time. I've been lenient thus far, but your attitude has to change."

It's true—he really has been lenient. He even gave me a full two weeks off after the accident. But despite all that, as I stare back at Mr. Avery now, I just shrug.

He gives me a disapproving look. "At this time, I have to give you a written warning." He slides the acknowledgement over to me.

"Awesome," I mutter sarcastically. I study the paper for a moment before picking up a pen and scribbling my signature. "Are we done?"

"That's it for now."

Before Mr. Avery can say another word, I'm out the door. As I'm walking back to the front, I spot McKenzie's father, John, who notices me and heads my direction. I suck in a deep breath.

"Hey there, Kelsey."

"Um, hey John." I try to smile.

"How have you been?" he asks.

"All right," I say simply. My gaze falls to the tile floor. *What's wrong with me?* I've never been this awkward around McKenzie's father before.

"What time is your shift over?"

"I'm off at six."

He smiles a little. "Well, Delia is making chicken parmesan if you would like to join us for dinner."

I stand there, silent. I used to go over for dinner all the time, always for chicken parmesan. It would feel so weird to go now.

"If you—" John starts.

"I'll come," I interrupt.

Even John looks surprised. "Oh. Okay. Great. Then we'll see you tonight," he says and leaves.

Why did I just say that? I haven't seen them since the funeral. My mom mentioned they've been asking about me at church. That's no surprise. The Fosters were my second family, after all.

When my shift is over, I buy tiramisu for tonight's dessert and head over to the Fosters' place.

On a normal day, I'd walk in without knocking. McKenzie and I would watch television, or if school was in session, we'd pore over homework while dinner was cooking. Now, I just stand awkwardly at the door, dessert in hand. From the little window beside the door, I see John pass by. He happens to glance up and notice me.

When he opens the door, he says, "You look lost."

"I wasn't sure if I should knock," I mumble.

"You never knock."

"Yeah, but that was before…"

"We'll figure this out. Come on in." John steps aside and I walk in. I place the tiramisu on a side table and offer to help. John and Delia gratefully accept.

When dinner is ready, I help set the table, and we all take our seats. John sits at the head of the table, Delia to his right and I to his left. McKenzie always sat at the end opposite her dad. I try to ignore the empty chair, the absent place setting. Delia bows her head to say grace, and John and I follow suit. While she prays, I just stare at my lap. After we each make up a plate, we eat in silence. The only sounds are forks scraping on plates and our chewing.

Delia is the first to break the silence. "So, are you excited for dance camp? That's coming up next week, right?"

"Oh, um…I decided not to go."

"I thought camp was supposed to be a time for you to bond with the team. You are still planning on being part of the dance team, right?" A flash of worry crosses Delia's face.

"I am. I'll meet the girls at the first rehearsal. Camp wasn't a requirement." Not wanting to talk about dance or school, I casually change the subject. "What did you do today?"

"Well, we went to church. Then, I went for coffee after service with your mom and Mrs. Williams." Mrs. Williams is Justin's mom, the wife of our youth pastor and leader of the women's Bible study.

"Oh," I say. "How was that?"

"It was good." Delia pauses. "Mrs. Williams asked about you. She said she hasn't seen you at church lately."

At that moment, I realize the topic of church is worse than school or dance. Maybe I should have kept answering questions about dance camp.

"Yeah, I haven't felt like going." I study my plate, wondering what my mom said during their chat today.

"Mrs. Williams told your mom if you ever want to talk, she's available. I can give you her number—"

"I don't need her number. I don't want to talk!" I slam my fork down and push away from the table.

"Oh, Kelsey, I'm sorry. Please sit," Delia pleads, her voice rough.

"No. I should go. Thank you for letting me come over. I'll see you later," I say, trying to keep my voice even.

"Kelsey, please—"

"It's fine. I'm fine. I should really get home, though." I get up and grab my keys. When footsteps follow me to the door, I turn to see John. Beyond him, Delia is trudging upstairs, her shoulders shaking. Guilt pricks at my conscience. I really shouldn't have snapped like that.

"I'm sorry," I say to John.

"It's okay. Are you sure *you're* okay?" he asks, voice laced with genuine concern.

"Yep," I say curtly.

"Will you do me one favor and let us know when you get home? I don't think you should drive while you're upset, but…" He pauses. "Thank you for coming."

My gaze wanders to the now-empty staircase. "I don't know if it was a good idea."

"She'll be all right," he assures me.

I meet his eyes. "Will you let her know I really am sorry?"

He nods. "Drive safe."

"I will. I'll text you."

Just as promised, I let the Fosters know when I arrive home safely. I know what it means to them. I take a few deep breaths before walking through the front door.

"Hi, sweetie," my mom calls out. "How was dinner?"

"Fine," I say as she rounds the corner.

She stops, examining my face. "I'm here for you if you want to talk about anything," she offers gently.

"I hear Mrs. Williams is also available," I snip.

"Yes, she did mention she hasn't seen you at youth group. She just wanted to let you know she's here. It's been a tough couple of months." My mom's words are tender, un-accusing.

"Tough is an understatement."

My mom tries to pull me into a hug, but I push away.

"Kelsey—"

"No. I don't want a hug. I don't want to talk. I just need…" *McKenzie*, my mind screams. "I need space."

I march into my room and slam the door. As I throw myself on my bed, hot tears flow freely. I miss McKenzie. I miss her so much, it physically hurts. Now, school is starting in less than two weeks, and I'll be going alone.

I flip over, staring at the cardboard back of a picture frame, and cry harder. I couldn't bear to look at the photo anymore, of me and her on the first day of senior year. We are holding an oversized cardboard sign that reads "SENIOR YEAR!" in giant white letters. When I got home from school that day, I printed two copies of the photo, purchased two identical frames, and gave one to her.

"Senior year, baby!" McKenzie exclaimed as she placed the frame on her bookshelf, right next to the stuffed bear I'd won for her at a carnival in junior year. "I am so ready to graduate."

"Me too," I said, sitting down on her bed.

"Can you believe we only have ten more months?" McKenzie asked.

I shook my head.

"Freedom," she said, plopping down next to me. "Then, college."

"Which will be awesome. You and I will be roomies, hopefully," I said, crossing my fingers. "Facing college life together."

"You and I against the world," McKenzie declared.

"Forever." I smiled.

Forever is a lie. I'm not ready to begin this journey, not without McKenzie. I turn away from my nightstand, squeezing my eyes shut until tears soak my pillow.

When I open my eyes, it's still dark outside, my light is on, and I'm still in my work uniform. I crawl off the bed and stumble to the bathroom. In the mirror, I notice my eyes are red and puffy. I quickly change into my pajamas, wash my face, and grab my phone to check the time. At the top of the screen, there's a voicemail icon. From Delia. I shut my phone off without tapping the voice message. I don't want to listen to it right now. More importantly, I don't want to hear any other messages I have saved.

After heading down to the kitchen to grab a snack, I sink into the couch, flipping on the TV. The channels are only playing infomercials, which always seem to suck me in. I watch actors demonstrate the new Wonder Mop until I finally drift off to sleep.

I dream McKenzie is alive and we're heading off to college. A gash mars her forehead, but there's no blood. I ask her what happened, and she shrugs, bending to pick up a box. As soon as she touches the cardboard, she winces and grabs her left wrist. When she examines it, the wrist is bent at an odd angle. She stares at me with wide eyes, her expression twisted in horror. But she can only see out of her right eye. Her left eye has swollen shut.

I gasp, waking myself up.

Three

It took me a full week to finally listen to Delia's message apologizing for the dinner fiasco. Though I called her back, I haven't returned to their house. With only one week left before I leave for school, I focus on packing.

I am folding my clothes into a moving box one afternoon when I come across a gray maxi skirt McKenzie let me borrow. I clutch it to my chest. This skirt. I was supposed to wear it to the Memorial Day party.

"See, I told you. It looks so much better on you," McKenzie said with a touch of sass.

I rolled my eyes. "Whatever. It looks great on you."

"Yeah, but on your slender dancer frame, it looks gorgeous. Who knows? Maybe you'll catch Brandon's eye." McKenzie winked.

"Don't be ridiculous. He doesn't even know I exist." I felt a blush rising on my cheeks.

"He will when he sees you in that. You'll walk out onto the patio, and Brandon will notice you. He'll stop what he's doing and come

over and say, 'Hey Kels. You look fine. Wanna grab a soda?'" Her voice dropped an octave to imitate his voice.

I laughed. "In what universe?"

"You never know. It's the little things."

I ended up not wearing the skirt. I'd be setting up for the party anyway, which meant I'd be all sweaty. I could wear the skirt and impress Brandon another day.

I gather myself, tossing the skirt in the box and rubbing my watery eyes.

I barely notice when Shelby walks into my room. "Hey Kelsey, want to go see a movie today?"

"Not now," I tell her.

"Later?"

"Shelby, I'm a little busy," I snap.

Looking hurt, she runs out and starts to wail.

"Shelby, what happened?" my mom asks, coming up the stairs.

"She's mad that I won't go to a movie with her," I call from my room.

She pokes her head through the doorway. "Kelsey, you can take a break. Everything doesn't have to be done today."

"I don't want to go to a movie," I grumble, looking up from my packing to glare at her.

"She just wants to spend time with you before you move."

"Seriously? You're going to guilt trip me?" I clench my jaw, annoyance bubbling up inside me.

"No, I just think it will be good for you two to spend some time together," she explains, her voice calm despite my rising volume.

"Well, I'm busy and I don't want to go."

"Kelsey, I understand you are going through a difficult time right now, but that is no excuse to take that tone with me. If you don't want to go, that's fine, but lose the attitude," she says, placing her hands on her hips.

"Sorry," I grumble, unable to erase the edge in my voice.

My mom doesn't say anything. She saunters away to check on Shelby. I hear bits and pieces of the muffled conversation. My parents decide to take Shelby to the movie later, leaving an invitation open for me to join. I don't end up going, instead shutting myself up in my room and continuing to pack. Eventually, I come across the bed sets McKenzie and I had purchased for our dorm.

"What about this?" McKenzie asked, holding up a quilt with a hideous floral print.

"No, we're not old ladies," I giggled. "This would be better." I unfolded a My Little Pony *comforter.*

McKenzie snickered. "If we're five." She turned down another aisle to browse the selection. "In three days, we will graduate high school. Can you believe it?"

"I am so ready for this. I can't wait to be in college, to be an adult," I said.

"I know. We're not kids anymore."

"Exactly the message that princess bedding sends when we show up to the dorms." I hold up a set of pink princess sheets, examining them.

"Yeah, I guess we could go with these instead." McKenzie rounded the corner from the next aisle over, holding plain beige sheets. "These say 'grown up.'"

"Boring! Maybe we don't have to grow up that fast."

"Agreed," she said, crinkling her nose.

When moving day finally arrives, I gather up my bookbag and some snacks for the car ride up when Shelby comes tramping down the stairs.

"I don't want to go," Shelby whines. "She isn't going to miss me. She's been mean to me all week."

I sigh, rubbing my temples. It's true, I have been snapping at Shelby a lot this past week, but it has nothing to do with her. I'm saying goodbye to my room, my house, my family. I'm heading to college alone—without McKenzie.

"She is going to miss you. You have to come say goodbye," my mom tells her. Shelby doesn't respond. I hear the garage door opening and footsteps in the foyer.

"We all ready?" my dad asks.

"I believe we are," my mom says as she enters the kitchen, Shelby following close behind.

They both stare at me, as if waiting for me to say something. I glance around to make sure I'm not forgetting anything. "Sure," I mumble.

Inside, I am freaking out, wishing we could give this whole thing up and stay home. Who really needs college, anyway? But I suppress my anxiety, grabbing my backpack and purse and heading for my car. As I slide into the driver's seat, Dad, Mom, and Shelby climb into the other vehicle. They follow behind me on my way to change my life completely.

When we arrive at Northern Arizona University, the parking lot is full. The campus is brimming with freshman students and their families arriving in cars packed with moving boxes, bedding, and lamps. Once we're parked, I get out and stretch. The trip here felt like the longest car ride of my life, and it was only three hours.

We leave my bags in the car so we can get the lay of the land, find my room, and make sure everything is in order before unloading. As we approach the registration office, my phone buzzes.

Happy moving day, the text from Delia reads.

I click my phone off and stick it back in my pocket, feeling a pang in my chest. Delia was supposed to be here with McKenzie. It should have been all seven of us on this new adventure, moving our stuff into the dorms.

There's a line at the registration table. The girl in front of me is chattering to her parents about how big the campus is and the classes she's excited about. When we fall in line behind them, the girl's mom turns to us.

"I don't know about you, but I'm a bundle of nerves. This one"—she points to her daughter—"can't wait for us to be gone. It's hard to let your baby go, am I right?"

My mom smiles politely. "Sure is."

I stare at the concrete, not saying anything. I'm hoping the woman doesn't try to ask any questions. Unlike her daughter, I'm *not* excited about being here. If I could skip college altogether, I would. Luckily, a spot at the registration table opens, and the family steps forward. Soon after, it's our turn. The younger woman manning the table greets us cheerfully. "College is going to be awesome. Are you ready?" she gushes.

I just blink back at her.

"Nervous?" She softens her tone, pausing. I still can't bring myself to say anything. "That's okay. It's only natural. So, what's the name?" she asks. My mom pipes in with my name, shooting me a disapproving look, and the woman thumbs through a tub full of manila envelopes, finally pulling one out.

"Here we are, Kelsey Lanter." She continues to talk, but I'm not paying attention. I crane my neck to glance around. The campus is practically a city. I have no idea how I'll ever find my way around.

My eyes fall on Shelby, who is still pouting. I know I've been mean to her the last few weeks, but I seriously am going to miss her. I nudge her foot with mine. She glances up, then shuffles farther away. Feeling a tinge of disappointment, I bring my eyes back to the table, a frown tugging at my lips. I try to listen to the conversation my mom and the woman are having. Then, I feel a nudge on my left foot. I look over to see Shelby glancing up at me from the corner of her eye. She's not smiling, but the pout is dissipating. I tap her foot back and then take a step closer, holding out my hand. She takes it. After thanking the woman, Mom turns back to us.

"Enjoy NAU, Kelsey," the woman at the desk says, waving at me. I simply nod in response.

After taking a seat at the nearest bench, my mom flips through the papers in the envelope. She pulls out the campus map and the keys. She also pulls out the dorm assignment, and I see a list of names printed on it. I tear my eyes away, too nervous to find out who my roommates are.

"Oh, that's not far," my mom says as she stuffs most of the papers back into the envelope. "Let's make sure the key works before we start unloading." She gets up and leads the way. The rest of us follow, and Shelby holds my hand the whole walk.

My dorm is in the Tinsley building. Pine trees tower around the three-story, red brick structure. A welcome banner hangs over the entrance. Once we're inside, we fight our way through the crowded halls. Through a few open doors, I see students and families unpacking boxes, hanging decorations, and getting beds made. In one of the rooms, two girls are hugging and jumping up and down. The sight makes my heart ache, and I avert my gaze. That should have been me and McKenzie.

We soon find my dorm room, and the key unlocks it with no hassle. The room is small with two beds, one in each corner. There's a desk for each of us and a small fridge against the wall. The door to the shared bathroom is on the opposite wall. Four girls, one bathroom. If we all have classes at the same time, getting ready is going to be interesting, to say the least.

The room is empty, no moving boxes or luggage. I assume my roommate isn't here yet. I didn't talk to her before the move-in date, so I have no idea what bed she wants. Choosing the bed on the far wall, I set my stuff down and just hope she'll be fine with my choice. Our next step is to start hauling in boxes, which takes us a few trips. Once we are unpacked, my mom decides I need a couple more things—a lamp for the desk, a pencil organizer, and some snacks for the fridge.

"All right, should we head over to the store?" Mom asks as Dad steps into the hall.

I shuffle my feet. "I think I'm going to stay and get situated."

"Are you sure? This is stuff for your room, after all."

"Yeah, I'm sure," I say, forcing a smile.

"Okay. Shelby, come on." My mom stands at the door, but Shelby doesn't budge from where she sits on my bed.

"I want to stay."

"Honey, I think Kelsey needs some—"

"She can stay," I cut in.

My mom studies my face for a moment, seeming satisfied. "We'll be back soon." She gives a little wave, closing the door behind her.

Once we're alone, I sit next to my sister. "Shels, I'm sorry for being so mean to you."

"Okay." She shrugs.

"I am really going to miss you."

"It doesn't seem like it," she whispers.

"I am! So much. You're my favorite sister."

She smiles. "I'm your *only* sister." We're both quiet for a minute. "Hey, Kels?"

"Yeah?"

She hesitates. "Was Tenzie supposed to be in that bed?" We both look over to the empty bed.

"I-I don't know. I didn't look," I stammer.

"I really miss her," she murmurs.

"I do too." I pull her into a hug. After a long embrace, I let her go and drag my feet over to my desk. Hesitantly, I pick up the room assignment page and glance down at the names. The girls who are sharing a room are in bold. The other two are the girls who will be sharing the bathroom.

My name is in bold. With my heart in my throat, my eyes wander to the second bolded name. I see the first three letters of my roommate's name, and my heart stops. *McK.* I read the rest, releasing a breath of relief. *McKenna Ritter.* The other girls are Amanda Kelly and Samantha Whitly. Of course my roommate's name has to begin with the same letters as McKenzie's. It almost feels like a cruel joke. With mixed feelings tumbling inside me, I sit back down next to Shelby.

"My roommate's name is McKenna," I say.

Shelby stares back at me. "That's a pretty name."

Not wanting to dwell on the topic, I ask, "Hey, you want to take a picture?" She smiles and nods. I grab my phone and open the front camera, snapping a picture of us. Thinking for a moment, I send it to Delia.

My parents return with more stuff than what was on the list. By dinner time, my side of the room is complete, and we are famished. My roommate never shows up. I glance over at the empty bed. I know it will be full soon, but a small part of me hopes she dropped out. I would honestly be okay with having the room to myself.

Our family decides on Chili's for dinner. Once seated in a booth, my mom is a fountain of questions.

"What's your schedule like?"

I take a bite of my burger. "Full."

"Are there any classes you're excited about?"

I shake my head.

"Are you anxious to meet your new roommate?"

I shrug.

"Did you look at your dorm assignment? Do you know who your roommate is?"

I swallow my bite. "I checked it while you were out shopping. Her name is McKenna."

"How exciting. Maybe she'll be there when you get back." My mom's tone sounds hopeful.

"Maybe." I take a sip of my soda. Suddenly, I'm not that hungry.

"Do you think you have everything you need for your dorm room? Maybe you can make a list, and we can do one final run before we leave tomorrow."

My dad sneaks a glance at me, then turns to my mom. "Hon, why don't we just finish dinner and get some rest? Moving has me beat."

"Moving is always tiring," my mom agrees.

I smile at my dad. *Thank you*, I mouth. He nods.

My parents drop me back off at my dorm before retreating to their hotel for the night. When I enter my room, there's a girl standing in the center wearing a teal tank top and a black mini skirt. She is leaning over a box, searching for something. When I walk in, she swings toward me, jostling her straight blonde hair.

"Hi there. I'm McKenna. Kelsey, I presume."

I simply nod.

"Awesome. Well, I see you are all set up." She nods toward my side of the room.

"Yeah. I hope that's okay. I didn't know what bed you wanted."

"It's fine. I don't really care. I'll set up the rest of my stuff when I get back."

When you get back? I think to myself. *You just got here.*

"Do you want to join me?" she asks with a sassy smile.

"For what?"

"There's a big beginning-of-the-year bash at Craig Matthew's house. It's supposed to be fun."

"Who?" Like it makes a difference.

"He's a senior—a friend of a friend. Anyway, who cares? It's a party!"

I grin politely. "No thanks."

"Suit yourself." She grabs her purse and keys and struts out the door. "Nice meeting you," she calls as she walks out.

"You too," I call awkwardly as the door closes behind her.

I look around the room, and my eyebrow twitches. When I left, the room was clean, but now, boxes are piled in the corner, with a few open boxes scattered on her bed. I wonder how long she'll be out. Probably late, if she's going to a party. It's also a college party, so there will most likely be alcohol.

Exhausted from the day, I decide to get ready for bed. Thankfully, the bathroom is empty. The last thing I want is to make small talk with anyone. I crawl into bed and check my phone. Delia has messaged me back.

Looks beautiful. Wow, Shelby has gotten so big.

I know. It feels like she will be here soon. She needs to stop growing, I reply. When I look at the picture again, it feels so empty without McKenzie wedged between us. Whether we were roommates or not, we would have spent the whole day together, helping each other set up our rooms. Our families would have gone out to dinner together. Once our parents left, we would have lounged around in one of our dorm rooms. McKenzie would have called Justin to let him know she was all settled in, and when they'd start getting mushy with each other, I'd probably make gagging noises until she gave me a pointed look. She would have made an audible kissing sound to him before saying she loved him and hung up. I sigh at the impression of what could have been.

I really miss my photographer, I type to Delia. *She would have documented this day way better than me.*

She would have filled up a whole memory card or two.

My screen blurs as tears fill my eyes. Suddenly, I'm glad my roommate isn't here. I curl up under my covers and let the tears fall on my pillow. With thoughts of my best friend playing in my mind, I cry myself to sleep.

I am woken up by the door rattling. It's still dark outside. I grab my phone, my thumb poised above the emergency button. The door opens, and I let out a tiny squeak before realizing it's just my roommate. She stumbles in, flipping on the light. I squint under the sudden brightness.

"Hey, sorry. Were you sleeping?" McKenna slurs.

"Yeah," I snap.

She grabs the desk to steady herself. "You can go back to sleep. I'm going to bed."

She disappears into the bathroom. The light is still on. I think about getting up and turning it off, but McKenna will probably need it to get to bed. She shuffles back in, throws her clothes on the floor, and sprawls on the mattress, the light still on. I wait there, still sitting up in my bed. Is she going to turn it off? Her breathing slows, and she falls asleep. With a huff, I get up and turn off the light, feeling my way back toward my bed. It takes me a while to fall asleep again.

My sleep is restless, like it always is in a new place. I'm facing the wall beneath my rumpled covers when I hear McKenna stir. I don't turn around. Just as I'm beginning to drift off, she heaves. I scrunch my face and clasp my hands over my ears. Maybe I'll have to start wearing headphones to bed.

Four

When my alarm clock goes off, I hit snooze and just lie there. I'm still drowsy and stiff from tossing and turning, but my parents are coming by this morning. Like it or not, I have to be up. I drag myself out of bed and shuffle to the bathroom, passing by McKenna who's sprawled out over her bed in a deep slumber. There is another girl at the bathroom counter getting ready for the day.

"Hi, I'm Amanda," she says cheerfully.

"Kelsey," I respond, setting down my toiletry bag.

"How was your first night?" she asks.

"Crappy," I answer honestly, not bothering to ask about her night.

"I'm sorry. How is your roommate?" She's clearly not catching the hint that I don't want to talk.

"Drunk," I say as I squeeze toothpaste onto my toothbrush.

Amanda half pouts. "Aw, did she go to the bash at Matthew's house?"

"Yesh," I say through a mouthful of toothpaste. How did everyone know about this party?

"I heard it was fun. I cannot wait to go to parties. I couldn't last night because my parents were here."

I nod.

"So, what are you looking forward to? Are you hitting up any parties?"

"Nope," I grumble, snatching my bag off the sink and heading back to my room. Yeah, I am definitely not in the mood for small talk.

My mom sends a text when they reach the campus, and I meet them outside.

"How was your first night?" my dad asks as I reach them.

"Sucky," I say.

"Did your roommate ever arrive?" my mom asks.

"Yes, then headed straight for a party."

"Oh." She exchanges a look with my dad. "Did she seem nice?"

"Sure. The sound of puking in the wee hours of the morning is going to make for a great friendship," I growl. My mom gives me a disapproving look. I sigh. "Look, I didn't get much sleep last night. I didn't get to know my roommate, so I don't know how nice she is. I *do* know she likes to go to parties and is into drinking, apparently. So, if we are done with all the questions, can we just get on with our day?"

My dad clears his throat and asks calmly, "Breakfast?"

"Yes," I say, starting for their truck.

"Do you need anything else for your room?"

"Another lamp," I mutter.

"We got you a desk lamp," my mom says, brows scrunched in confusion.

"Yeah, but that one is bright. I need a dull one or a nightlight if my roommate is going to be barging in late. I would prefer not to be blinded every time she comes in. That way, she can see without leaving the room light on all night."

"Well, that sounds like a good idea," my dad says.

"If she continues to do this, you need to tell your RA," my mom chimes in.

"Yeah, okay." I fight the urge to roll my eyes.

After breakfast, we stop at Target for another lamp, and I pick up a couple more things before we return to the dorms. McKenna isn't in the room when we get back. Once we've set down the shopping bags, my mom double-checks that I am all set. I can tell she's hesitant to say goodbye. When it's time for them to leave, she gives me a tight hug, and I see tears in her eyes as she pulls away. I try not to look at her. Instead, I focus my attention on Shelby, who is staring at the floor. I crouch down, waiting for her to look at me. Finally, I tuck my finger under her chin and lift her head.

"I don't want to say goodbye," Shelby whimpers.

"Neither do I," I tell her. She wraps her arms around my neck and I pull her in tight, a warm tear trailing down my cheek. "This is not goodbye," I whisper into her ear, my voice cracking in my tight throat. "This is just see you later." A tear hits my bare shoulder.

"I don't want to leave you," she says, gripping me tighter.

"I'll be home before you know it." I try to stand up.

"Promise?" she asks, loosening her grip.

"Yes. Plus, you can call me, and we can Facetime."

"Okay," she mumbles, wiping the tears from her cheeks. "You can call me too."

"I will." I smile as fresh tears gather in my eyes. I blink hard to push them back. "I love you."

"I love you too," she says, planting a kiss on my cheek. She inches back and grabs Mom's hand.

"Call often," my mom tells me.

"I will. I love you."

"Back at you, sweetie," my mom says. My dad gives me a final hug, and then they're gone.

Exhausted, emotionally and physically, I crawl back into bed and doze off again. When I wake up, McKenna is unpacking boxes, a coffee cup on her desk.

"Hi, did I wake you?" she asks.

"Not now," I snip, still annoyed about last night. "I bought a lamp. I can leave it on at night so you don't turn the light on."

"Ah, sorry about that." She sips her coffee. "I usually don't drink much, but sometimes it's good to unwind."

I bite my tongue, not replying.

"You should come out with me sometime," she offers.

"No thanks," I say curtly, picking up my schedule to look at my classes.

"What classes are you taking?"

"English, photography…" I stop reading. Originally, McKenzie and I decided we would each take a class to explore each other's passions. NAU had a dance team, which I had tried out for and been accepted into, but there were no recreational dance classes on campus. I had looked up dance studios nearby and found one that offered classes for all levels. We decided hip-hop would be fun. Meanwhile, I had enrolled in a beginning photography class. I don't want to take photography without her, but I'm not sure what I'd replace it with. I study my schedule. Is it too late to change it?

"Are you a photographer?" she asks.

"No," I say, not wanting to elaborate.

"Guess it's good you're taking the class then," she quips.

"Uh-huh." I glance up at her. "What about you?"

"Your basic beginning classes—math, English, biology, psychology, and labs."

"That's a lot of sciences."

"Yeah. I've thought about going into nursing, which requires a lot of science."

"Cool," I say, tucking a messy lock of hair behind my ear.

"I guess. We'll see how it goes." She shrugs.

The first dance team rehearsal is on Tuesday evening. I step into the dance studio, feeling instantly at home. The far wall is lined with mirrors, and dance barres snake through the room. Several of the girls greet each other and hug. Camp must've been a great bonding experience. When I find the coach, Ms. Oliver, I introduce myself. She smiles and says it's wonderful to have me, then gathers the rest of the girls to begin the session. To start, the team introduces themselves. There is one other girl who didn't attend camp, which makes me feel a little better.

Rehearsal is long and strenuous. I didn't keep up with workouts and practice like I should have over the summer. By the time I make it back to my room, my legs are burning. It's going to take some work to get back in shape.

After a few weeks my muscles are growing used to the rigorous practices. It's a Saturday night, and I'm spending it slouched at my desk staring at the mound of books and weeks' worth of notes—or lack thereof. What can I do? I barely have motivation to make it to class, let alone do my homework. I have already skipped several classes this week, and if I keep this up, I'm sure I'll be dropped. Ms. Oliver pulled me aside during rehearsal last night to let me know if I wanted to stay on the dance team, not only did I have to maintain a five-class schedule, but also keep at least a 3.0 GPA. If my academic performance didn't improve, I would be dropped from the team.

McKenna saunters out of the bathroom. Her hair is smooth, her makeup immaculate. I know the drill by now. She has been working hard at her desk all afternoon. Now, it's time to go out.

I shuffle over to my bed.

"Giving up?" she asks, grabbing her purse.

"For tonight."

"Want to join me?" she asks, just like every other weekend. And like every other weekend, I decline.

"Suit yourself," she says, walking out the door.

The next weekend I'm stretched out on my bed, laptop in front of me, trying to catch up on homework. McKenna has already left for the evening. I take a small break for the weekly check-in with my family. I speak with Mom first. She tells me she took the liberty of looking up a few churches close to campus. I roll my eyes, but don't say anything.

"Honey, I think it would be really good for you," she encourages.

"Mom, I'm just focused on school right now."

"I know, but there are other things in life besides school." It's silent for a moment. "After everything with McKenzie, I know it was hard for you to attend service. I just thought it might be easier up there. There wouldn't be so many memories."

I don't answer. She thinks I didn't show up was because there were too many *memories*? What about the fact that God didn't do anything? The line is silent.

"I won't push. Just think about it?"

"Yep," I say curtly.

She says goodbye and then passes the phone to my dad and Shelby. Once I hang up, I finish my assignments and head to bed, preparing for classes on Monday. After Ms. Oliver's warning about being kicked off the dance team, I make sure I am present for each class. I can tolerate most of them, though there is one class I hate—photography.

Listening to the lectures, I can just imagine McKenzie sitting beside me with her eyes glued to the professor, soaking up everything she could, even in a beginner's course. Photography was always her thing; it was never mine. Most days when I attend, my chest aches and I feel like I can't breathe, but I just go so at least the teacher can mark me as present. I lay my head on my desk and start to drift off.

"Hi. Kelsey?" a voice says above me.

"Yeah." I sit up and look around. Most of the class is already gone. Before me stands a boy, his lean build matching his five-foot-seven frame. His button-down shirt and cargo shorts give him that typical college-boy look, and his chestnut brown hair is spiked in front. I'm drawn to his big brown eyes, which seem warm and kind.

"I'm Matt, your photography partner," he explains.

"Partner?" I ask, feeling completely lost.

"For the photography project," he says. My oblivious face must expose that I have no idea what he's talking about because he continues, "We have to get to know a classmate and then present an introduction of them using pictures."

"Oh," I say, vaguely recalling the last few words of our lecture and hearing the professor say *partner*.

"Yeah. We need to use the techniques we'll be learning in class."

"Awesome," I say with a sarcastic edge, packing up my notebook. Great. Working with a partner makes it harder to slack off, and Matt doesn't look like the type to shirk his homework.

Matt follows me out the door. "So, how do you want to do this? I mean, we have a few weeks to complete it, but I don't think we should wait until the last minute."

"I don't know," I groan.

"Well, why don't we exchange contact info, and we can meet up later this week?" he suggests.

"Fine." I cross my arms as he pulls out a piece of paper. He writes down his phone number and email and hands it to me. I write my phone number on the bottom of the page, rip it off, and give it to him.

"I'll text you later," he says, walking away. I shove his number in my bag and drag myself to my next class. McKenzie never leaves my mind. If she were here, she would be trying to set Matt up with me. After all, he is pretty handsome, just a bit taller than me with beautiful eyes.

That evening when I return to my dorm room, I pull out the photography syllabus. Sure enough, our final is a group project using the techniques we learn in class to introduce our partner. Poor guy. He has no idea who he just got stuck with. The moment I sit at my desk and crack open my math book, McKenna marches in and drops her backpack on the floor. "Biology sucks!" she exclaims, plopping down on her bed.

"Sorry," I offer.

"I cannot wait for the weekend," she says as my phone buzzes. I glance down to see a number I don't recognize.

Meet Thursday in the library, it reads. This must be Photography Guy. What was his name again? I can't recall, so I save it in my contacts as Photography Guy.

What time? I have rehearsal at 8, I text back.

We can be done before 8.

"Hot date?" McKenna asks.

"Nope." I sigh. "Just a photography project."

By Thursday, I've brainstormed several excuses as to why I can't make the meeting. A cold, a family emergency, maybe a quiz I forgot about. The text conversation glares at me on my screen, waiting for me to type. In the end, I can't go through with it. I pop out of bed and head to the library at the last minute. I'm already late, so I pull my hair into a ponytail as I walk. At the library, I spot Matt and head his way. He notices me, and I catch him giving me a once-over. I glance down at my outfit—dance shorts and a loose top, nothing special.

"Hey, how's it going?" he greets me.

"Okay, I guess."

"Cool. So I was thinking today we could spend some time getting to know each other, and then over the next several weeks we can take all the pictures we need." He looks up at me, waiting for a response.

I shrug.

"Do you have a different idea?" he asks.

"Nope. Your idea is fine," I say, pulling out a chair.

"Okay. Well, how do you want to do this? Should we ask each other questions or just share a little bit about ourselves?"

"Questions are fine," I say, an edge creeping into my voice.

"Okay." He hesitates, clearly taken aback by my attitude. "I can start."

"Super," I retort, unable to shift my sour mood.

He takes a breath, looking down at his paper. "Where did you grow up?"

"Arizona, down in the valley."

"Cool. I grew up in Gilbert."

I nod, jotting down his response.

"Do you have any siblings?" he asks.

"Yes, a sister."

"Is she older or younger?"

"Younger. What about you?" I ask. He pauses. He opens his mouth and then closes it, as if carefully thinking over how he is going to answer. I didn't think the question deserved *that* much thought.

"An older brother and a younger brother," he finally says.

"Is your older brother in college?"

"Nah, he's, um, he's… " Matt fidgets in his seat.

"Pursuing other things?" I suggest. I get it, not everyone takes the college route.

"Sure, we'll go with that." His face pleads for me to not ask any more questions, so I drop the subject. We're both silent for a moment.

"So, why photography?" Matt asks.

The question catches me off guard. *Because of McKenzie!* I want to scream. *Because she loved photography. Because that was our deal.* Instead, I keep my mouth clamped shut. The thought of McKenzie sends a sharp pain through my chest. I bite my lip, trying to make it look like I'm pondering the question and not about to burst into tears. "I don't have an answer for that one."

"You said you had rehearsal. Rehearsal for what?" Matt asks.

"I'm on the dance team."

He shoots me a charming smile. "That sounds fun. You guys perform at the games?"

"Yep." I nod.

"Which is your favorite?" he asks. "Between photography and dance?"

"Dance," I say quickly.

"How long have you been a dancer?"

I breathe a sigh through my nose. "If you ask my mom, since the time I could walk. I started lessons when I was five."

"That's a long time. I bet you're really good."

"I do…all right." I smile despite myself. "What about you? Why photography?"

"I've always looked at photos and thought how cool it would be to capture my own. I finally decided to take the leap and join a class."

"Do you like it?"

"So far, yeah. You?"

I shrug, not wanting to let my true feelings spill over. The notes I've written in my notebook begin to blur. I clear my throat and quickly rub my eyes. "Anything else?" I ask impatiently, ready for this conversation to be over. Ever since he asked why I decided to pursue photography, I can't get McKenzie out of my head.

"I think that's it," he says politely. "We should take some time to think of some deeper questions. If we want to ace this, we need to prove we really know each other, not just surface details."

Yep, just what I thought. Definitely not a slacker.

Matt clears his throat once he sees my less-than-enthused expression. "I know it's a lot, but I think it will be good. I've heard Mr. Jacobs likes the students who go above and beyond."

Except, that's the problem. I don't want to go deeper. I'm good doing the bare minimum. I've *been* doing the bare minimum up until now. But this is his grade too, and I'm not going to ruin it.

"Okay," I say reluctantly.

When I get to the dance studio, my thoughts are still on McKenzie.

"Kelsey, smile!" Ms. Oliver shouts over the music. I do my best to plaster on a smile and stay on the beat. Ms. Oliver glances at me, clearly not satisfied. She has yelled at me twice tonight. I finish the routine off-beat, and she shakes her head in disappointment.

After our meeting, I try to come up with deeper questions to ask Matt now that I finally learned his name. Up until today, his number was still saved as Photography Guy. I glance up from my English assignment to see McKenna getting dolled up for a party tonight, like usual.

"You sure you don't want to come? I bet it will put you in a better mood. You've been mopey since Thursday."

She's asked every time. And honestly, what's the worst that could happen? Before I think better of it, I blurt out, "Sure."

McKenna's eyes widen, a surprised smile on her lips. "Okay!"

Stowing my homework, I brush my hair out and get changed. It's just jeans and a tank top, but I'm more dressed up than I've been in weeks. McKenna offers me her flat iron, and I run it over my hair and add a little makeup.

"Wow, you look good," she compliments.

A blush creeps onto my cheeks. "Thank you."

Am I really doing this? This is my first college party after all, and there is bound to be alcohol. The more I think about it, nerves start to crawl in, but also a feeling of exhilaration, something I've not experienced in months.

Five

We walk to the party, which is only a block off campus. When we step in, the house is crammed with college students. Someone calls McKenna's name the moment we enter, and she leaves my side immediately. Not knowing what to do, I wander into the kitchen and grab a soda. I spot a few people I know from classes. One guy from my math class watches me as I walk back across the living room.

I find a spot by the wall, sipping my soda. What am I doing here? I never go to parties. The only reason people party is to hang out with friends and drink, and I don't have friends here or drink. But after I finish my soda, I vow to myself to try something stronger. Maybe that will dull this excruciating ache that's been constricting my chest ever since Matt's "why photography" question. I've already had a few drinks when McKenna waves me down.

"Hey, hey. Looks like someone is more relaxed. See, it's good to get out and let loose."

I nod, though I'm not sure I feel better. Dizzy is more like it.

"Told you it would help, didn't I?" She gives my shoulder a nudge.

I just shrug.

McKenna turns to her group of friends. "I told her she needed to get out. Jeez, she's been moping in our dorm room for weeks." She lowers her voice. "Like someone died."

"Someone did," I snap, crunching up my plastic cup as I draw a fist.

McKenna stands there, wide-eyed.

"My best friend, who should be my roommate—she died. So, I'm sorry that I'm lame and boring. I'm sorry that I'm a dud and you don't like me. But if you ask me, you shouldn't be the one who…" I stop myself.

"The one who what?" McKenna crosses her arms and glares at me.

"You shouldn't be my roommate. It's not how any of this was supposed to go. It should be reversed. McKenzie should be my roommate, and you should be…"

McKenna's mouth drops open. "Are you saying I should be dead?"

"Yes—I mean, no," I slur, my mind fuzzy from the alcohol.

"Okay, that's enough," one of the guys next to her says, fixing me in a hard stare. "I think you need to leave."

"Gladly," I say. When I turn, the room spins. I take a few steps before stumbling into someone.

"Hey, are you okay?" the stranger asks.

"Yeah," I mumble, trying to sidestep the partygoer and reach the door, tripping in the process.

"Woah, let me help you." The voice sounds like it belongs to a guy.

"I'm fine." The room is still wavering around me.

"No, Kelsey, you're obviously not."

How does this person know my name?

"I'm fine, really," I say, trying to pull myself away. In the process, I lose my balance and nearly fall backward.

"Yeah, you're perfectly fine." Whoever it is takes my arm and wraps it around their shoulder. I notice the slight, yet muscular build. Yep, definitely a guy. We begin to head for the front door.

Once outside he asks, "Do you know where your dorm is?"

"Of course," I start to say—until darkness swirls around me.

When I open my eyes again, I'm in a bed, but I have this strange suspicion I'm not in mine. I try to get my bearings straight, but when I roll over, my stomach does a somersault. There is no way I'll make it to the bathroom in time. Leaning over the side of the bed, I hurl into the small trash can next to it, bitter stomach acid burning my throat. When I finish, my head is throbbing.

"How ya feeling?" the voice from last night asks. When I lie back down with a groan, the door opens, letting in the light from the hall. I squeeze my eyes shut as the throbbing in my head intensifies. The door clicking shut seems to burst my eardrums.

"Sorry," a female voice whispers. It doesn't sound like McKenna. "Hey, she's alive. How's she doing?"

"She just threw up," the guy informs her. I'm more with it than last night and the guy's voice sounds extremely familiar. I just can't quite place it.

"Yeah, she did that a few times last night," the mystery girl replies. "Hopefully it's out of her system now."

I threw up last night? I carefully open my eyes. The room is dark except for a desk lamp. A poster of some actor is plastered on the wall.

I look down, running my hands along the navy blue sheets that are definitely not mine. Whose room am I in? I sit up slowly.

"You good?" the guy asks, and now I'm positive I know who's asking.

"She looks green," the girl comments.

"Deep breath. You're okay," the guy says.

"I don't feel okay." My voice sounds raspy. When I dare look up, I see a girl I don't know and, to my horror, Matt. Great.

I moan, burying my head in my hands as my stomach does another somersault.

"Do you need some water?" the girl asks.

I shake my head, not looking up. A nauseating pain crashes through my skull from the movement. I suck in a deep breath, still feeling like I'm going to vomit. Lying back onto the soft pillow, I close my eyes. I must doze off, because when I wake again, it's to the sound of a television laugh track. Matt and the girl are sitting on the other bed with a laptop in front of them.

Matt glances up. "Hey. Hungry?"

"Uh, I don't know." Honestly, I still feel queasy.

"I bet you'll feel better once you eat." Matt hops off the bed and jogs out the door.

"Hi, I'm Heather." The girl waves from the bed. Now that I can focus, I notice Heather has auburn hair and appears to be an inch or two shorter than I am.

"Kelsey," I say. "Sorry about last night."

"It's okay. Is this a regular thing?" she asks.

I shake my head. "This is a first."

"Ah, okay. Thought so."

"How did I get here?" I ask, glancing around the room.

Heather cocks her head. "How much of the night do you remember?"

"I remember going to the party, finally grabbing a drink, and hanging out on the patio for a while…" I try to recall more, but my mind draws a bunch of blanks.

"I wasn't at the party, so Matt will have to fill in the rest for you. He brought you here because he didn't know where your dorm was." Didn't I tell him? I vaguely recall him asking. Did I not answer?

"You said I puked several times." I cringe at the fresh memory.

"Oh, yeah. Don't worry, though. Matt missed most of it. You know, curfew and all."

"Great." We're both quiet for a minute. "What time is it?" I finally ask.

"Quarter after one," she answers.

The door opens, and Matt walks in alongside another guy, both of them carrying bags of takeout. The new guy is sporting navy blue Converse All Stars and has his short, dirty blonde hair spiked. He struts over to Heather and gives her a kiss, then turns to me. "Hi. I'm Jake."

"Kelsey." I wave awkwardly. The smell of chili powder, cumin, and cooked meat makes my stomach growl, but I'm still not sure I can keep anything down.

"Let's let these two catch up," Heather says, hopping off the bed and grabbing a takeout bag. She heads for the door, and Jake follows her out.

"Want a taco?" Matt asks, sitting on the floor near Heather's bed. I slowly climb down. His eyes are still trained on me as I join him. "You doing all right?"

"I think so," I lie, my head still pounding and my stomach rolling.

Taking my words at face value, Matt hands me a taco. I just stare at it, debating whether to take a bite. What's the worst that could happen? Answer—I might throw up in front of him again. I take a bite, nibbling cautiously.

"So, no dance performance this weekend?" Matt asks.

"Away game," I say.

We eat our tacos in a comfortable silence. Matt was right. I do feel a little better with food in me. I ask for another taco, and he hands me a soft shell. After swallowing the first bite, I ask, "Do you think you could fill in the blanks from last night for me? I don't remember much beyond getting a drink."

"Let's see… You and your roommate—I'm assuming she's your roommate—got into a little altercation. Then, you turned to leave and ran into me. I walked you out and asked where your room was, but you were out of it, so I brought you to Heather's room. I knew her roommate was out of town so there would be a bed."

"Thanks," I say, still trying to piece the night together.

"So, can I ask you a question?" Matt asks, hesitant.

"Sure," I say, though his serious tone puts me on edge.

"Who's McKenzie?"

I freeze, unable to speak. I've already puked in front of him. I don't need to cry in front of him too.

"Do you remember why you got into an argument with your roommate?" he asks.

I rack my brain, but it's all a blur. But between bits and pieces, I think I told her she wasn't supposed to be my roommate.

"Kind of," I mutter.

"You implied she should be dead and McKenzie should be here instead," he says quietly.

"I said that?" That doesn't sound like me.

"Yeah, you said that." He takes a sip of his soda. "So, who's McKenzie?"

Tears well up in my eyes unbidden, and one escapes down my cheek. I rub my eyes, willing the tears to stop. It's not working.

"What happened?" he asks, as if he already knows the answer.

"She was in an accident," I whisper, my voice catching. The tears come harder. Her face flashes through my mind—her eye swollen shut, the stitches etched across her forehead. The image stabs my chest, and once again, I struggle to breathe.

"She didn't make it," Matt says solemnly. A statement, not a question.

Unable to speak, I simply nod. This conversation hurts too much. I went to the party because of this, because I was tired of thinking about her, of feeling this pain.

"I'm so sorry," he whispers.

I hug my knees and bury my head in them, letting the tears fall. I try to stop crying, but I can't. I haven't cried this hard since the first week after the accident. Across from me, Matt shifts and sits back down next to me. Once the tears stop flowing, I lift my head. Matt is looking at his phone, a box of tissues situated between us. I grab one and blow my nose.

"Sorry," I say, clearing my throat.

"Do you want to talk about it?" He glances over at me.

I open my mouth, then close it again. This isn't the first time I've considered talking to someone, but I just can't. It hurts too much. Eventually, even if I don't talk about it, all this hurt, this anger and sadness, will fade away. Right? "Not really," I finally say.

"I know you don't know me that well, but if you ever need to talk, I'm a good listener."

"Thanks." Neither of us speaks for a while. I fiddle with my thumbs until I finally ask, "So…now what?"

The last thing I want is to go back to my room and face McKenna, but I can't stay here. I also feel disgusting and want to wash last night's grime off me.

"What do you want to do?" he asks.

"Shower," I say automatically.

"Got it. Let me walk you to your dorm." He offers a hand to help me up.

Before leaving I tie up the trash bag containing the vomit and leave some money for laundry, along with a little note with my number. I drop the bag into one of the larger trash cans in the common room. There we find Jake and Heather. Jake sees us and waves.

"You leaving?" Heather asks.

A grateful smile crosses my face. "Yeah. Thank you so much for letting me crash. Sorry again for last night."

"It's cool. Crash anytime, preferably sober though." She grabs a scrap of notebook paper, jotting something down before bouncing over to us. "My number." She beams.

"Thanks," I say, tucking the paper in my pocket.

"I'll be back in a few," Matt tells them. "Just going to walk Kelsey to her dorm."

"Cool. See you soon." Jake looks over at me. "It was nice to meet you."

"You too."

The moment we step outside, the wind howls across the neatly trimmed lawn. When another guy brushes past us and yells to his friend, the sudden noise makes me wince. Matt casts me a worried glance. Recovering, I scan the area to figure out which direction to walk. But everything is a little too familiar. I swing around and glance up at the building we just came from.

"Um, *this* is my building," I say.

Matt chuckles. "We were so close. What floor?"

"Third," I say. "What floor is Heather on?"

"She's on the second."

Heather and Jake are bent over one of their phones, so they don't notice when we walk back inside toward the flight of stairs. The glare of the lights still hurts, and heavy bass streaming from one of the rooms chips away at my brain.

"Lots of aspirin and water," Matt comments. "Mac and cheese is good too."

"Thanks for everything," I say, shooting him a smile.

"No problem."

I stare at my door, trying to muster up the courage to open it.

"Something wrong?" Matt asks.

"Would you want to face your roommate after something like this?"

"Good point. Maybe she's not here."

As the last words leave his mouth, the door swings open, making me jump. McKenna and a girl from the party fill the doorway, glowering at me. I step aside to let them out. As they pass, the girl utters a few profanities, some directed toward me. McKenna glances back and nods.

"I guess I deserve that," I say as I walk into my room.

"Don't let it get to you. Apologize and move on," Matt advises, standing in the doorway.

I sigh. "I guess I'll see you tomorrow at class."

"Yep." He turns to leave.

"Thanks," I call out again, feeling that I can't say it enough. He turns back and winks. Smiling, I close the door.

Six

Come Monday morning, I head to photography class earlier than usual.
I can't stand being in my dorm room anymore. When McKenna
returned yesterday night, I apologized for what I'd said at the party.
She ignored me, stomping to the bathroom and slamming the door.
When she came back out, she immediately put her earbuds in and
didn't remove them until she went to bed. I tried to talk to her again
before I left, but she just grabbed her earbuds and continued to study.

"Hey, how are you?" Matt jolts me out of my spiraling thoughts as
he walks up to me.

"Water and aspirin work wonders," I say.

"Good. Mind if I sit here?" He points to the chair next to mine. I
shake my head.

"So, I tried to apologize," I say as he sits.

"And?" He raises an eyebrow.

"Well, I'm here early."

"Didn't go well, I take it?"

"It didn't go, period. She refuses to speak to me." I groan,
massaging my temples.

"Do you blame her?"

I sigh. "No."

"She'll come around," he says encouragingly.

"Not any time soon," I murmur as the professor begins the class. I try to pay attention today. I want to do well on our project, especially to help Matt. When class is over, Matt and I make plans to meet on Friday afternoon to continue getting to know one another. Instead of heading back to my dorm after classes, I meander over to the library to work, then grab dinner at the dining hall before returning to my room. I hold my breath as I open the door. Thankfully, McKenna isn't here. I let out a sigh of relief.

Coffee? the text from Matt reads.

Yes please! Large vanilla latte, I respond. *I'll pay you when you get here.*

Twenty minutes later, there's a knock on my door. When I open it, Matt is holding two cups of coffee. "For you," he says, handing me the large cup.

"Thank you," I say, truly grateful for the caffeinated drink. Between schoolwork and McKenna being completely disrespectful when she comes home in the evening, I have been getting very little sleep. At first, she just ignored me. But as the days went by, she started trying to be as loud as possible. She no longer uses the lamp I bought and instead turns on the light. If I get up and turn it off, she turns it on again when she exits the bathroom. She claims the lamp is too dim and she can't see with it—even though the lamp was perfect last week. She also makes a point of slamming drawers and doors shut. Needless to say, the week has been miserable. Friday couldn't have come soon enough.

"You look exhausted," Matt says.

"You have no idea," I grumble. I'm about to fill him in on the drama when McKenna walks in. She marches over to her stereo and turns it on, then sits at her desk. Matt glances over at her.

"Do you mind turning that down?" I ask politely. McKenna doesn't say anything. She powers on her computer and pulls out one of her textbooks. "Please, we're trying to study," I add.

"You don't look like you're studying," McKenna retorts.

"We're about to get started. Can you please turn it down or put on headphones?" I ask, my tone still level. Matt glances between us.

"No," she answers defiantly.

"Just for now." I try to quell my irritation.

"If you don't like it, leave."

"It's my room too," I say, raising my voice.

"Does it look like I care?" She glares at me, her face hard. I stand anyway and turn the volume down. All she does is storm over and crank it up louder.

"Seriously?" I ask, spinning on my heel, about to turn it off completely. She ignores me.

Matt gets up and grabs his backpack, heading for the door.

I wheel around to face him. "Where are you going?"

"*We* are going to the library," he answers. "Grab your stuff."

"Matt, we don't have to leave. McKenna can turn down the music." From the corner of my eye, I see McKenna's blonde hair wave as she shakes her head.

"She doesn't have to. Let's just go to the library."

"But—" I begin, but Matt shakes his head subtly. Huffing, I pack up my backpack and we walk out. I close the door behind us. "We didn't have to leave."

"I know, but it looked like it was going to turn into a fight, and there doesn't need to be."

"I have every right to be there!" I say, louder than I intended.

"Kelsey, don't yell at me," he says defensively.

"I'm not." I bring my voice down.

"Is this how it's been all week?"

"Pretty much," I pout.

"Keep trying. It's not going to get better overnight. Let's be honest, what you said was not the nicest."

I sigh. "I know, but I was also drunk."

"I understand that. You hurt her feelings, though."

"Then she needs to talk to me!" My voice rises again as my resentment boils over.

Matt gives me a patient smile. "Maybe this is her way of letting you know how she feels," he says. "Not that I agree with what she's doing."

"It's just so frustrating, and I am freaking tired."

"I hear ya. I remember my first year—my roommate was horrible."

"First year?" I ask, tilting my head.

"Yeah, I'm a sophomore," he explains. "Hang in there. Next year, you get to choose your roommate."

"That is so far away," I groan as we make our way toward the library.

The place isn't bad for studying, but when you have to carry a conversation, people nearby give you dirty looks. Matt and I try to find a table in a back corner, though there is one girl who's within earshot. Every now and then, she glares at us.

"So, what do you like to do on weekends?" I ask.

"I don't have much of a chance to do what I like. Right now, it's just homework and church on Sundays."

"You go to church?" I ask, slightly surprised.

"Yeah, Sunday mornings."

I nod, making a note.

"Have you ever been to church?"

"I used to go all the time," I answer, not elaborating.

"Haven't found a church up here yet?"

"Haven't even looked," I say simply.

"If you ever want to join us, you're more than welcome," he offers.

"Who's us?"

"Jake, Heather, and me."

"I don't know," I mutter, fidgeting with my pen. The conversation with my mom comes to mind. I shove those thoughts aside and focus on our project.

The rest of the afternoon, we chat about the project, his family, my family, the rest of the classes we are taking, and our hobbies. The sun is setting when we finally leave the library. During our conversation, Matt never revisited the "why photography" question nor asked any questions about McKenzie, for which I was thankful.

"If you want to join us on Sunday, you're welcome to," Matt says.

"Thanks." I doubt I will ever take Matt up on that invitation. We say goodbye, and I head straight for rehearsal.

The question of going to church lingers in the back of my mind alongside thoughts of McKenzie. After her death, the only time I stepped into a church sanctuary was for her funeral. I'd made it clear while praying in that hospital chapel—if He took her, I was done. And I've kept my word.

Thinking of McKenzie also makes me think about John and Delia. Since starting college, I've barely spoken with them. I send a quick text to Delia as I head into the dance studio. After rehearsal wraps up, I see she responded, so I call her on my way back to the dorm and complain about my roommate woes.

"It's only been a few weeks. I'm sure the two of you will work things out. Living with someone is always an adjustment," she says in an encouraging tone.

Yeah, it's even worse when you get drunk and tell her she should be dead, I think sarcastically. That *really helps things along.* I unlock the door and enter a dark room. McKenna must be gone again.

As I reach for the light switch, I hear a noise. I pause and listen. A guy's voice. McKenna giggles, and then the bed creaks. Sure, it has only been a few months, but she has never brought a guy to our room before. I don't want to be here for this. Quietly, I close the door and head for the common area. Maybe there I can get some homework done.

When I arrive, the room is packed with students chatting and laughing. I sigh, heading downstairs to try the first floor. There, only one lonely soul is working on homework. I sit at a table and pull out my English book and my notebook. I absentmindedly rub at a bruise on my left shin—thanks dance rehearsal—while I work. It's getting late, and I'd rather be in my room asleep. I yawn, trying to focus on my homework when I hear laughter from behind me.

"Kelsey?" Matt asks, looking confused. I turn to find him, Jake, and Heather walking in.

"Hey, you survived your hangover," Jake comments.

Heather pops up behind him. "Wait, you live in this building?"

"Um, yeah." I push my English book aside.

"What are you doing down here?" Matt asks.

"Well, you know how it was heated between me and my roommate earlier?" I start. He nods, and I add, "She's taken it to another level."

"What's wrong?" Heather's glance flits between me and Matt.

"What did she do?" Matt asks.

"Not what. *Who*," I say, raising my eyebrows.

"She has a guy in your room?" Heather asks, incredulous. I nod.

"What are you going to do?" Matt crosses his arms.

I shrug. "Nothing."

"You can't do nothing. Technically, she can't have a guy in the dorm after ten and, hey, look at that. It's after ten," Heather says, holding up her phone.

"I think you need to tell your RA," Matt adds.

"You saw how it was earlier," I say, exasperated. "Telling someone will only make things worse."

"Yeah, but this crosses a line." He draws one in the air with his finger for emphasis.

"Is it really that bad?" Heather asks.

"It's pretty bad." Matt shoots her a telling look.

"Look, it's fine." I yawn. "I'll figure something out."

"What dorm number?" Heather asks.

"Why?" I ask, looking at her skeptically.

"Number," she demands.

"Three-five-three," I say, packing up my books.

She starts for the stairs.

"Wait— Where are you going?" I shout to her retreating figure as Jake starts to follow. "Where is she going?" I ask Matt, who's still standing beside me. The look on his face gives me the answer.

I rush up the stairs, catching up to her halfway to my room.

"What are you doing?" I ask as she stops and pounds on my door.

"I'm getting you your room back," she says.

"Let's just leave it alone," I hiss. "I'll be fine for a night." Matt joins us as Heather bangs her fist on the door again. The door cracks open, and the guy pops his head out.

"What?" he asks with a huff.

"This isn't your room," Heather states defiantly. The guy stares back at her and scoffs. He starts to shut the door but Heather holds her arm out to stop it.

"What is your deal?" the guy growls.

"This is not your room and you don't have permission to be here, so I think it's time for you to leave," she says.

The sound of movement tumbles from the room, and McKenna swings the door open wider. She spots me behind Heather and shoots me a death glare.

"Seriously? You're pathetic! What, couldn't stand up for yourself so you get someone to do it for you?"

My cheeks grow hot. "I-I didn't ask her to do this."

"You are such a baby. Maybe it's a good thing that friend of yours isn't here. At least she's saved from the embarrassment of being your friend." She pauses to glance at Heather before her eyes bore into mine. "Oh, wait. Let me guess. Your friend was your backbone, and when she died, you lost it. Bet she'd be happy you found a replacement. Now, tell me, is this one better?"

Tears spring to my eyes.

"Aw, what's the matter?" McKenna asks in mock pity.

"Stop!" I snap. A hot tear rolls down my cheek. The guy who was with her walks back in the room, re-emerging with his shirt on and shoes in hand.

"I think I'm going to take off," he says. McKenna turns to him.

"You don't have to. Just stay. She can figure something out." She fires me another icy glare.

"I'll hit you up later," the guy says before disappearing down the hall.

"You happy now?" McKenna barks before muttering a profanity under her breath.

"Excuse me?" Heather says, looking offended.

"Nothing. This doesn't concern you," McKenna bites back. "Well, now that my company is gone, I guess you can come in." She steps aside, but I don't move. She scoffs. "This is what you wanted, isn't it?"

I'm seething with barely repressed anger—about everything. I'm angry with McKenna for being a jerk in the first place, with Heather for stepping in and making things worse, with myself for getting tongue-tied, with McKenzie for not being here. I draw a deep breath in an attempt to calm myself.

"I think I'm going for a walk," I grumble.

"Super. You scare off my guest, and now you're not even staying," McKenna says with an exasperated eye roll.

"I'll be back in a few minutes," I snap.

"Whatever." McKenna slams the door, leaving Heather, Jake, and Matt standing there as I grind my teeth, angry tears pooling in my eyes.

"Kelsey?" Matt says quietly.

"Don't even start!" I shout, storming toward the stairs. Matt yells for me, but I don't turn back. I thrust the door open and walk outside.

"Hey, can we talk?" he asks just behind me. He must've run to catch up.

"No!" I stop so abruptly, he nearly bowls into me. "No, we cannot talk. I told you I would figure something out. I told you I didn't want to make things worse. I am very capable of taking care of myself! So why is Heather, who I have only met once by the way, just taking matters into her own hands? As if things weren't bad already, now look where we are! And McKenna talking about McKenzie that way? She had no right!" I shout in his face.

"You're right," he says calmly.

"You bet I'm right! So now, if you would kindly leave me alone, that would be amazing."

"Kelsey, Heather does that. She inserts herself into situations where she feels someone is being treated—"

"I don't need an explanation, and I honestly don't care," I snap. "Go home!" I turn and stomp down the walkway. This time, Matt doesn't follow.

I walk briskly, letting the tears stream down my cheeks. In my hurry, I left my jacket back in the common room, so I'm freezing by the time I get back to my building. I grab my jacket before heading back upstairs. When I open the door, the room is pitch black. I don't bother turning on the light, instead groping through the dark to turn my desk lamp on. Gathering my pajamas and bathroom bag, I glance over at McKenna's bed. She is under her covers, sound asleep. I get changed quickly and crawl into bed.

When I wake on Saturday, McKenna is already up and dressed. The tension is palpable. Any time I try to talk to her, she ignores me. Realizing my efforts are futile, I give up and get ready for my dance performance at the football game.

Later that evening, my mom calls for her weekend check-in. When she asks if I've thought about church, a groan slips out. She immediately changes the subject. Heather tries calling a few times as well, but I send her to voicemail.

Before I know it, Sunday rolls around. I look over my photography project and consider getting ahold of Matt, but I'm still too ticked off to talk to him. I abandon the project when my stomach starts to growl. As I'm walking to my car to pick up dinner off campus, I hear my name. I turn to see Heather rushing to catch up to me.

"Hey, I tried calling you this weekend," she says when she reaches me.

"I know," I say, an edge creeping into my voice.

"Oh." Her gaze falls to the ground. "I just wanted to apologize."

"Okay."

"Look, I shouldn't have stepped in. I should have respected your feelings and left it alone."

I nod, my jaw clenched.

"Anyway, I really am sorry. How is it going?"

"Well, it's been pretty quiet ever since. We haven't spoken to each other."

"I'm sorry," she says with a small voice.

I just shrug, not in the mood to talk.

"Have you talked to Matt?" she asks.

"No," I say, staring down at my shoes. "I'm just mad right now."

"I get that. Don't freeze him out for too long, though."

I breathe a chuckle through my nose. "Well, I can't for too long or we'll fail our assignment."

She stuffs her hands in her pockets. "So, where are you headed?"

"I was going to grab some food."

"Me too. Want to join me?"

I hesitate before deciding that company might not be a bad idea. "Sure."

Heather smiles, and breathes a subtle sigh of relief. "Cool. I can drive. I know just the place."

Seven

Heather brings me to a hole-in-the-wall Chinese restaurant tucked in the corner building of a shopping center. The patio is decorated with paper lanterns, and lights shaped like lotus flowers line the low iron fence. Inside, the room is painted a deep red with gold dragons snaking along the accent walls. On the back wall, an outline of an ancient Chinese gate surrounded by cherry blossom trees finishes the authentic look. I gawk at the mural, admiring the golden sunset beyond the gate. We order our food and find an empty booth. For a moment, the sounds of bustling servers and chatting diners fill the silence that stretches between us.

"So, how's college?" Heather asks. I cringe at the awkward question.

"Okay, I guess," I say, slouching in the booth.

"I know you're in photography with Matt, but what other classes are you taking?" Heather asks.

"I have communications, French, dance rehearsal, English 101—"

"With Mr. Rueben?" Heather asks.

I nod, leaning forward. "Monday and Wednesday."

"Tuesday and Thursday," Heather says, smiling at the connection.

I smile too. "So, what are you going to college for?" I ask as an employee sets our food down. Steam rises from the plate, and the tangy aroma makes my mouth water.

"I want to be a counselor or a therapist. I feel like I'm a good listener."

I give her a pointed look, raising an eyebrow.

"When I'm not jumping in to make a situation way worse than it already is. Did I mention I'm sorry?" She smiles apologetically.

"Yeah, you did." I grin, twirling some noodles around my fork and taking a bite. "Oh my gosh."

"Right? It's *so* good." Heather beams as she takes a bite from her own food. "I wish I could take credit for finding it, but the guys found it. Anytime we want Chinese, we come here."

Heather and I pause our conversation to eat. I'm glad I accepted Heather's offer for dinner—I had no idea what I was missing. "How long have you and Jake been together?" I ask when my plate is clean. I lean back, feeling the bulge in my stomach.

"High school. He was a senior; I was a junior."

"How did you meet?"

"At a school assembly." Heather snorts. "He was seated in the row in front of me. He and Matt were whispering nonstop. I eventually tapped Jake on the shoulder and politely told him to pipe down, and he rolled his eyes. They did stop talking, though. When the assembly ended, Jake turned and made some sort of sarcastic remark. I don't remember what it was, but of course I retorted. We saw each other in the halls from time to time after that. It took him a while to ask me out, but we've been together ever since. I think Matt was jealous when I came around." Heather giggles.

"Yeah, best friends can be that way," I say, recalling how I felt when I found out about McKenzie and Justin.

"He got over it eventually." She pauses to take a sip of her soda. "What about you? Any guys in your life?"

"Nope, not since high school. That relationship only lasted a couple of months."

"Well, new school, new guys. College guys are supposed to be better, or so I hear. I really don't know."

I breathe a sigh through my nose. "Maybe. Right now, I just need to focus on passing my classes."

"I hear ya there," she says.

When we get back to campus, she reminds me to get ahold of Matt. After squeezing me in a hug, she starts for her room. She makes it two steps before turning. "We should do this again sometime."

I smile. "Yeah…for sure," I say, waving as she leaves. And surprisingly, even to myself, I mean it.

Back in my room, McKenna is at her desk studying. I quietly set my stuff down and sit at my own desk. She doesn't say anything and neither do I, but the silence is at least an improvement from the offhand comments and rude glares over the past couple weeks.

When I get to class on Monday, Matt is already in his seat. I slide into the seat next to him, wondering if he'll say anything to me. His eyes remain glued to his phone.

"Hi," I say, trying to break the ice.

"Hey," he replies politely, not looking up. The professor walks in, and I reluctantly turn away from Matt to watch the lecture. Once class is over, I hastily gather my things. But somehow, Matt is up, his backpack packed, before me.

"Matt," I say as he takes a step toward the door. He turns to me, his face giving away no emotions. I clear my throat. "Can I talk to you?"

He doesn't reply, but he also doesn't walk away. It's a start. "I just wanted to say—" I stop myself. To be honest, I don't know what to say. Yes, I'm sorry for yelling, but I also feel it was justified. Nothing was his fault, though; he was just trying to help. Matt is still waiting, so I murmur, "Thanks for trying to help."

He nods.

"I saw Heather last night," I comment, hoping to lighten the mood. He raises an eyebrow, intrigued. "We got dinner at Lou Mings."

The change of topic works. "What did you think?" he asks.

"It was delicious. I'll definitely be eating there again." I feel a flutter in my stomach when he finally smiles.

"Jake and I found it our first year here." He leans in conspiratorially and whispers, "They do takeout too."

"They do?" I ask, excited at the prospect of chowing down quality Chinese food in the dorms.

"Oh yeah," he says enthusiastically. We meander toward the door. "So, do you have any time this week to work on the project?"

"I think I have Wednesday free."

"I can do that. We can meet in my room, if you want."

I grin. "Sounds good."

On Wednesday, nerves roil in my stomach as I walk to Matt's dorm. This is the first time I've been in his room; I expect it to smell like a guy room—whatever that smells like—with dirty clothes piled on the floor and takeout containers everywhere. But when he opens the door and I step in, I'm pleasantly surprised by how tidy it is. It even smells clean and fresh. My face must show my surprise since Matt explains, "Jake hates clutter." I just glance around, nodding. Not bad. The door opens again, and Jake and Heather walk in.

"Hey!" Heather lights up when she sees me. "How's your paper coming?"

"It's not," I say with a playful grimace.

"Oh, I know. I am completely stuck," she groans, plopping down on Jake's bed. "I can't believe it's due in two weeks."

"Which teacher is this?" Jake asks, taking a seat next to Heather.

"Mr. Rueben," I say.

"Ooh," both boys say in unison.

"He is tough," Matt says, cringing.

"Yeah, I almost had to retake that class because of him," Jake remarks.

Heather and I look at each other worriedly. "This is *really* encouraging, guys," Heather says.

"You two will be fine. You are so much smarter than me," Jake says, patting Heather's knee.

"If you took Mr. Rueben, let me see your paper. Just for some inspiration." Heather gives Jake a pleading look, but he shakes his head.

"You'll be better on your own, trust me." He kisses her forehead.

Heather suddenly points at me. "Hey, when is your next dance performance?"

That catches both boys' attention.

"The next game is Saturday."

"I'd love to see you in action," Heather says. Jake gives her a quizzical look, so Heather explains, "She's on the dance team."

"Wow, that sounds fun," Jake comments.

"Yeah, it is," I mumble.

"Woah. Hold back some of your enthusiasm," Jake remarks with a sarcastic smirk.

"No, it really is." I try to sound more upbeat. It's true. Dance was the one place I could always breathe. The world melted away in the dance studio, where I'd practice for long hours. McKenzie would always make fun of me for being a perfectionist when it came to dance routines.

"Can you show us something?" Heather asks.

"Like what?" I stare back at her, blinking.

"A turn or a jump?"

I stand and do a pirouette. "How's that?" I ask, sitting back down.

"Beautiful! We should totally go to a game. I want to see my girl in action." Heather winks at me.

I give her a slight smile. "Just let me know when. Maybe I can get you tickets."

Jake groans. "All this work is making me hungry."

Heather laughs. "We haven't even started yet." But she sheepishly adds, "Food does sound good."

"I could eat," Matt says. He glances over at me, expectant.

"I am a little hungry," I admit.

"Lou Mings?" Matt asks, his eyes still trained on me.

"Dude, yes!" Jake practically shouts.

"I know you just had it, but after you mentioned it, I can't stop thinking about it," Matt admits.

"I'm good with it," I say, rolling my shoulders. From what I remember, their menu was extensive. It would be a while before I got sick of the food.

While Heather and Jake drive over to pick up the food, Matt and I get to work on our project. We'll need to start snapping photos soon if we want to make a dent in our project before Thanksgiving break. He sits at the desk, tapping his pen on his paper. I sneak a peek at the page he's focused on. It features a list of pictures he wants to take of me. While scanning the list, one particular word catches me off guard. We've already talked about all the pictures he wants to take, and he never mentioned snapping a shot of me dancing. I clear my throat and point to the word with my pen. He glances over at me.

"I just added it," he says.

"Do you really want one of me dancing?"

"Well, you said dancing was your favorite when we talked. And from the little turn I saw today, it seems like you're good at it."

"If you want, we can get that photo." A silence stretches between us as I study my own paper.

"Are you sure?" he asks.

"Yeah, dance is good. It's me."

I draw in a deep breath. Dance is me. Just ask anyone. Still, ever since the accident, I have a harder time getting into it. Dance is expressive, but lately I've been struggling to express what I'm feeling. All the songs in dance right now are happy or peaceful. I'm not feeling either of those emotions, and I'm not doing a good job at faking it, either. On several occasions, Ms. Oliver has told me, "This is a joyful sequence. Smile." I try, but smiling isn't in me right now.

"One more week," McKenzie squeals.

"I know. I am so ready for a long weekend of turkey, pie, and…"

"Rolls!" we finish together.

"So, what time should I be over?" I ask.

"We'll serve dinner around one. You're welcome over anytime, though." As she speaks, McKenzie's features blur before becoming clear. Her face is bruised, and a deep cut on her forehead starts dripping blood.

"What happened?" I ask, concerned.

"It was an accident," she says nonchalantly. "So, when are you coming by?"

"Wait, what accident? It looks bad," I say, examining the rest of her body. When my eyes return to her face, it's pale.

I wake with a gasp. Blinking, I catch my breath, afraid to close my eyes again. That's the fifth time since Wednesday. It's the same conversation every night, and each time, McKenzie looks pale, sometimes translucent. The nightmare always wakes me up and I know I won't be able to fall back asleep, so I get up and trudge to class, exhaustion tugging at my eyelids. I lay my head down on the desk as I wait for class to start.

"Rough night?" Matt asks, sitting next to me.

"Rough weekend," I mumble without lifting my head.

"What?" he asks.

"Rough weekend," I repeat, a little louder. Matt starts to say something, but I nod off. I wake up to the professor lecturing. I drag myself into a sitting position and notice Matt glance over at me. With horror, I realize drool is dripping down the side of my mouth. I wipe it off and try to pay attention to the rest of class. When class is over, I grab my backpack and stand.

"Everything all right?" Matt asks, sounding worried.

"Um…yeah."

"'Cause that convinces me," he says, rolling his eyes.

"I haven't been sleeping well. But I'm fine."

"Why aren't you sleeping well?"

"Don't worry about it." The truth is, I don't want to explain that I'm having nightmares about my dead friend. I head for the door.

"Is it your roommate?" Matt asks as we step into the hallway. "Has she had more guests over?"

I shake my head.

"Are you stressed about classes?"

"No…"

"Worried about going home?"

"Oh my gosh, no!" I snap. "Leave it alone."

He holds up his hands. "I was just trying to help," he says, looking hurt.

"Well, I told you not to worry about it. I'm fine. So just drop it."

"Fine, dropped." Matt averts his gaze, his jaw clenched. "I have to go. Did you want to meet this week?" His tone is sharp.

"I don't know. I leave Wednesday," I tell him.

"Okay. Enjoy your Thanksgiving," he says, attempting to sound polite.

"You too." I try to smile but give up, knowing my Thanksgiving will be anything but enjoyable.

Eight

Being home for Thanksgiving is nice. Unfortunately, because my grandparents and my aunt and uncle are in town, I have to share a room with Shelby. I want my own space, but sharing a room with my sister isn't all bad. She spends the whole first night telling me about her school year and the few sleepovers she's been invited to. I listen as she excitedly details everything. She is genuinely happy. I, on the other hand, feel suffocated.

Photography is a constant reminder of McKenzie. I feel her absence everywhere, and seeing her in my nightmares isn't exactly helping. When Shelby finishes her rambling, she asks me about school and if I have made any friends. I let her know how my classes are going, and I tell her about the few people I've met.

"Delia will be happy," Shelby comments.

"Why would she care?" I ask, surprised.

"She asks about you every time I see her at church."

"Oh." I fidget with my sleeve.

Hearing they are still going to church brings up a bitter resentment inside me. How can they go back there? God took their little girl from them; He took my best friend. This so-called God of love, of healing, of miracles, of answered prayers—He didn't do anything. He let her die.

"She misses you," Shelby whispers.

"I miss her too," I say, my heart aching. Guilt eats at me since I've only texted her a few times since the school year started.

"I miss McKenzie," Shelby whimpers, and it kills me. I wrap my arms around her and squeeze her tight.

"Me too," I whisper in her ear, trying not to cry.

Thanksgiving dinner is delicious. But ever since my conversation with Shelby, the Fosters are on my mind. I text Delia wishing them a happy Thanksgiving. For years, I would eat Thanksgiving dinner at McKenzie's, and then McKenzie would come to my house for dessert. Then, we would go out with my mom and aunt for Black Friday shopping. I skip it this year.

The rest of the weekend is quiet. I only have one nightmare, which isn't too bad, all things considered. When I walk downstairs in my pajamas on Sunday morning, my mom frowns.

"It would be nice to have you join us this morning," my mom says.

"I'm good. I'll see you guys after." I give her a smile.

"Kelsey, the whole family is going, and I know several people who would love to see you," she pushes.

"Okay." I walk into the kitchen and grab a package of Pop-Tarts out of the pantry. I turn to head back to my room. My mom follows with a pensive look on her face.

"Oh my gosh." I roll my eyes. "I'll make everyone late this morning. What if I agree to go when I get back to school?"

"You make it sound like it's torture."

I bite my tongue to keep from saying something that will most definitely escalate the situation.

"Honey, I think finding a church will be good for you. It will help you meet new people."

"I am meeting people," I say, feeling a little defensive.

"I know, and I'm happy about that, but I think it will be good for you to know people who have…similar beliefs," she says.

I don't say anything about Matt or the fact that he goes to church. Mentioning a guy who goes to church will spark a whole different conversation. "Okay," I say instead.

No one on campus seems to have energy after the holiday break. I know I don't. In fact, I can't wait for the semester to be over. Matt is already in photography class when I walk in and sit. He glances over at me but doesn't say anything right away, so I assume he's still upset about our conversation before the holiday.

"Hey, how was your Thanksgiving?" he asks.

I stare back at him, a little stunned. "Good, yours?"

"It was good. Lots of food."

"That's what the holiday is all about," I remark as the professor starts the class. He reminds us we have three weeks before our presentations.

"Hopefully," he adds, "you already have most of your pictures taken. I can always tell who waited until the last minute!" As he speaks, I remember that Matt needs pictures of me dancing.

"So, your dance rehearsal is on Tuesday?" Matt asks after class.

"And Thursday and Friday."

"Is there one day better than the others?"

I shake my head. "Not really. I already talked with our coach, so whenever is best for you."

The rest of the day, I try not to dwell on the idea of Matt watching me dance. My palms get sweaty just thinking about it. When I arrive on Tuesday, I'm relieved to see he's not there. Rehearsal starts, and we are completing our opening stretches when he walks in. I should've known he'd want to get the pictures as soon as possible. The coach gets up to talk with him briefly, nods, and then comes back to finish leading our stretches. Matt takes a seat in the corner and unpacks his camera.

I take a few deep breaths, trying to ignore his presence. My stomach is already in knots. After the stretches, we do a few floor exercises to warm up before moving into the routine.

"Okay, we're going to start this evening by practicing the middle section. Some of us were a little off on Saturday, and that will *not* be acceptable come competition," Ms. Oliver yells as she points the remote at the stereo, cueing the music. Everyone rushes to their places.

With the music blaring, I focus on the routine, trying not to think about Matt watching me. Ms. Oliver starts clapping to the beat, which means someone is off. "Kelsey, come on. One, two, three, four." The clapping continues for a few more beats. "Thank you," she calls out in a frustrated tone.

I catch a glimpse of Matt in the mirror, camera to his face. Heat rushes to my cheeks. This is embarrassing. I'm scolded two more times during the period Matt is snapping photos. A wave of relief rushes over me when he gives me a small wave goodbye.

The next day, I meet up with Heather and the guys. I walk into Mario's Pizza, spotting the three of them at a table. I pull out the last chair.

"So, I hear Matt got to see you in action," Heather says as I sit.

"Yeah. Did you get any good shots?" I ask, casting him a shy glance.

He smiles. "Yeah. You looked good out there."

I wrinkle my nose. "I could have been better."

"Can I see?" Heather asks excitedly.

"I don't have my camera," he says. "I can show you when we get back to campus."

"How long have you been dancing?" Jake asks, taking a bite of pizza.

"Since I was five." I grab a slice of pepperoni.

"Wow. That's a long time," he says, sounding impressed.

"My mom always jokes that I was meant to dance. I was twirling and skipping before she even put me in dance classes."

"Did you ever think about going to a specialized dance school?" Heather asks.

I take a bite of pizza, mulling over the question as the table awaits my answer. "I thought about it some, but McKenzie and I wanted to stay together. Plus, I'm not sure I want to be a career dancer. Though I have thought about teaching dance." I hang my head, eyes fixed on my plate. Just mentioning McKenzie brings a throbbing ache to my chest. The table is silent.

"How did your paper go?" Jake asks Heather, clearly trying to shift the mood. As she rants about the assignment, I look up to see Matt's eyes on me. I smile at him before focusing my attention on Jake and Heather. We are just finishing dinner when Heather snaps her fingers, pointing at Matt.

"Hey, Mrs. Miller needs your help moving some tables before church on Sunday."

He nods. "I can do that."

Heather turns to me. "Do you go to church?"

"It's been a while," I say.

"You should come with us sometime."

"Oh, I don't know," I say, mixed feelings welling inside me.

"It's a really great church. I think you'll like it."

I just nod. I still have no desire to go to church, but then again, joining my friends one Sunday might get my mom to stop nagging me about it.

When Friday comes, Matt and I are back in the library working on our project. Photos litter our table as we debate which ones to use. I pick up one photo that Matt took of me at rehearsal. The girl in the photo looks miserable. It's me, but also not. I sigh and set it down. Matt holds another picture, staring at it intently. I peek over—it's a picture I took of one of his framed photos. Matt and his brothers, Brent and Noah, are covered in mud, huge smiles on their faces.

"Do you miss them?" I ask.

"Every day." Matt's voice catches.

"You get to see them in a few weeks," I say.

Matt clears his throat. "Yeah." He sets the picture aside and picks up the one I was just holding. "Do any of these speak to you?" He motions to a couple of others from rehearsal.

"Any of them are fine."

"Fine is dangerous territory. You may say it's fine, but then when we do the presentation, you hate the picture. And then you hate me for choosing the picture." A small smirk pulls at his lips.

"Really, I don't care. Whatever you want."

Matt pulls two pictures toward us. "These are my favorites."

I study the pictures. One shows me stretching, and the other is a picture of me from behind, my reflection in the mirror. Both shots are professional-looking with an artistic touch. They remind me of photos McKenzie has taken. She would spend hours examining photos and editing them to perfection. If she were here, she would be impressed with these—especially the reflection piece.

"This one." I point to the reflection photo, my throat tightening. A tear slips down my cheek.

"You sure?"

"Absolutely. Really shows off your photography skills." Before I can stop myself, I add, "McKenzie would have used that photo. She may have done a few touch-ups, but there would be no hesitation. It's fantastic."

Matt sets it down in the pile, pensive.

"Is McKenzie the reason you took photography?" he finally asks.

My body tenses, and tears erupt out of nowhere. I press my palms to my eyes, willing the moisture away. I grit my teeth to keep from screaming as all my feelings from the past few months finally bubble over. I can't breathe, I can't move. I'm hyper aware that I'm in the library, surrounded by people who are probably staring at me, which makes the tears fall harder. I will my body to move, wiping my eyes, and notice a group looking in our direction.

"If you want to go, I can clean up," Matt whispers.

I nod, grabbing my bag and bolting for my car. When the door is shut, I release a guttural scream. Tears soak my lap, and snot runs from my nose. Will this pain ever end?

The next Saturday after the game, I stop by Matt's dorm to pick up my pictures. He doesn't mention my meltdown in the library.

"How was the game?" he asks casually.

"It was good. We won," I say.

"Cool, cool."

After grabbing my photos, I quickly retreat to my dorm. The temperature has dropped significantly, and I'm not built for the cold. I tell myself that's the only reason, not that I'm embarrassed seeing Matt again.

While I am hibernating in my dorm room, cuddled under my blanket, my mom calls. She asks about my plans for Sunday and reminds me of the agreement we made over Thanksgiving. I don't remember her agreeing, though I guess since she let me escape to my room, that was her way of solidifying the deal. Now I have to follow through on my end.

Before I can vet my words, I blurt out, "I'm going with my friend Heather."

"That sounds great." I can tell she's trying to keep her excitement in check.

When I hang up, I text Heather and let her know I'll need directions to the church. I sigh. There's no going back now. Heather responds with the directions and a little party popper emoji.

Nine

Sunday morning is bright and sunny. When I arrive, the parking lot is already packed. Behind the massive main building, I can make out a few smaller buildings and a playground. After hunting for a parking spot, I stride toward the largest building, pulling out my phone. I make it to the little courtyard in front of the church when I hear my name.

"Hey, glad you made it," Heather says, bouncing over to me and giving me a hug.

"Thanks." I smile, greeting Jake as he saunters up beside Heather.

"Let's go find a seat." Heather turns and skips inside. I follow silently. The lobby forms a half-circle, with a coffee shop tucked in the corner and a few tables out front. A few church members are milling around, chatting. Heather heads to a set of propped double doors, and we step inside.

The sanctuary is bigger than I expected. Two large screens hang down on each side, and four sections of chairs face the stage. Heather finds an empty row in a section to the left and takes a seat. I follow behind, my steps robotic. The service hasn't even started yet, and I already feel anger beginning to simmer.

"Hey, good to see you," Matt says, stepping in beside me.

"Hi," I say, trying to sound natural.

"How are you?"

"Okay." My answer is short, but that's all I can handle right now. I suck in a deep breath as the lights dim and the worship team climbs the stage. Most of the band members appear to be in their early to mid-twenties. The first song is upbeat. I don't sing along, I just listen. The second song is familiar, and it rockets my anger to another level. I ball my hands into fists and take a few more deep breaths. I make it through the first verse of "King of My Heart", and then the chorus starts.

I shake my head. I don't want to sing this—I don't even want to *hear* it. I tap Matt on the shoulder. He moves, and I storm out of the sanctuary. The door opens behind me, but I don't turn around.

"Kelsey, wait," Matt calls.

I whip around. "I'm not going back in there," I snap, a fresh wave of tears brimming in my eyes.

"Okay, sure. We can wait for worship to be over."

I shake my head. "It's not just worship, Matt. I can't do this. I can't be here," I shout. A couple heading inside glances over at us.

"Look, Kelsey, I get it…" he starts. I hold up my hand.

"Don't. I don't want to hear that you *understand* or that you *get it*. You don't get it. No one gets it!" I yell, turning toward the parking lot.

"Kelsey, can you please stay?" he calls after me.

"No!" I shout back, marching to my car. I half expect him to follow me, but when I reach my car, he is still standing on the sidewalk, looking hurt. Part of me feels bad, but how can he possibly understand what I'm going through?

I spend the afternoon running errands and working on homework before finally returning to my dorm. I grab the door handle to my building when someone barks my name. I turn to see Jake stomping toward me, his brows furrowed in anger.

"I believe an explanation is owed," Jake says.

It takes me a second to realize he is talking about this morning. I sigh. "Look, I didn't need an 'I'm sorry' speech. It's not like Matt could possibly understand."

"He does, though." He chuckles bitterly and shakes his head. "He lost his older brother a few years ago."

I inhale sharply. "Oh," I whisper.

"Yeah," Jake says. "He understands more than you know, so stop snapping at him. Stop thinking you're the only one who has ever lost someone."

"I-I didn't know," I stammer.

"Because you didn't listen to him or let him explain. You were so focused on *you*. If you're going to keep hanging out with him, with us, then you need an attitude adjustment."

"Okay," I say, looking at the ground.

"Okay," he says matter-of-factly. He walks away and I stand frozen, trying to process what just happened. It takes me a while to get my feet to move.

When I return to my room McKenna is at her desk, earbuds in. She glances over at me and pops one earbud out. "Your friend was here looking for you."

"Which one?" I ask, assuming it was Jake.

"Your photography partner. What's his name?" She pauses then snaps her fingers. "Matt."

"O-oh, okay." I blink in surprise. "Thanks for letting me know."

"Are you going to talk to him?"

"Later," I mumble, grabbing my pajamas and heading for the bathroom.

"He seemed like he really needed to talk to you," she adds.

"Why do you care all of a sudden?" I growl, my tone biting.

"I don't. He looked upset, and his voice made it sound urgent."

"Well, I appreciate the info," I say, closing the bathroom door. I walk back out in sweats and a long-sleeved T-shirt.

"Your phone rang," McKenna informs me. I roll my eyes but check my phone, seeing a missed call from Matt. After what Jake said, I have no clue what to say to Matt. Jake is right. I never gave Matt a chance to talk about his brother. Then again, he never mentioned it in our previous conversations, so maybe he doesn't want to talk about it. I grab my keys and jacket, shove my feet into slippers, and head for the door. McKenna glances over at me but doesn't say anything. When I get outside, I start toward Matt's building. About halfway there, I spot him walking a few feet in front of me.

"Matt," I call. He turns.

"Hey," he calls back. When I reach him, neither of us say anything.

Finally, Matt breaks the silence. "I know he told you."

I look up at him. His face is calm, but a spark of anger lingers in his eyes.

"Why didn't you tell me?" I ask.

"You were going through a hard time. I wanted you to have a chance to work through it. I know how difficult it is to have everyone tell you they understand, and worse is when they just want to tell you their story."

I lift one shoulder. "You could have told me."

"I tried today, but you stormed off before I had the chance."

"Sorry…"

"It's okay," he says. "Sorry for Jake, by the way."

"Why?" I ask, surprised. "He was just being a good friend."

"He has a big mouth."

"He was honest with me, though." I give Matt a pointed look. "Is it okay if I ask what happened?"

Matt is silent for a minute. He sucks in a shaky breath and releases it slowly. "Brent was in a boating accident. He and his friends went out to the lake one day…and another boat wasn't following the rules. They hit my brother."

I can't help but gasp.

"He was in the hospital for a few days. At one point, they thought he was going to make it. But then he got an infection, and his body was too weak to fight it. He died a few days later."

"I am so sorry," I breathe.

He sighs. "It is really hard to lose someone. I wanted to let you know I completely understood, but you were so upset, so I let you go. I was frustrated, though, and when Jake asked where you were, I kind of exploded on him. I guess he decided to take matters into his own hands. Sorry about that."

"It's okay," I say. "Wait, did he tell you he talked to me?"

Matt nods. "I saw him just now as I was headed out. He looked worked up, and I asked him if he and Heather had gotten into it when he told me he saw you."

"Oh."

"I tried to call you a couple of minutes ago to check up on you."

My lips lift in a half smirk. "You know you don't have to. I'm a big girl."

"I know. But you were really upset this morning, and then Jake yelled at you. Not a great day. I just wanted to let you know I'm here if you ever need to talk."

"Thanks." I smile at him. Until I remember the picture of his brothers from our time in the library. "Oh gosh…the photo assignment…"

"It wasn't easy," he admits. "I miss him a ton."

"So, you were just going to let me get up in front of our whole class and lie?"

"You're not lying."

I give him an incredulous look.

"I do have two brothers, and technically, Brent is pursuing other things. Heavenly things, but other things nonetheless." He cracks a smile.

"All right." I shake my head.

"So, do you want to talk about this morning?" he asks hesitantly.

I shrug. I haven't talked to anyone about my falling-out with God. I'm not even sure I *want* to talk about it.

"You don't have to," Matt adds when I don't say anything. "You just seemed mad this morning."

"Yeah, well, I am." Noticing my voice rising, I take a steadying breath.

"It's okay to be angry," Matt says.

"No, it's not."

"Who says?"

"I just got yelled at," I say pointedly.

"You just have to be angry with the right people," Matt explains.

"Well, those people aren't here, are they?"

He furrows his brows. "Who are you mad at?"

"I'm mad at God, and I'm mad at Mc—" My voice catches, and tears start pooling in my eyes. "McKenzie."

"Why?" he asks gently.

I just shake my head and rub my eyes. "I don't want to talk about this."

"We don't have to, but it *is* okay to be angry. It's also okay to let whoever you're angry with know. God can handle every emotion you're feeling."

I focus on my shoes and try not to cry.

"Do you want to go eat?" he asks.

I look up, blinking the moisture from my eyes. "Um, sure."

"I was going to meet Jake and Heather," he says as we stroll toward the parking lot.

I pause. "Is he still mad?"

"He'll be fine. I'll tell him we talked, and everything is good." He smiles at me. I nod in response and continue walking.

The next couple weeks fly by like nothing between studying and exams, which also means it's time to give our final photography presentation. I hustle into class and sit next to Matt.

"You ready for this?" Matt asks.

"I hate public speaking," I whisper. McKenzie always thought that was crazy since I could dance in front of a huge crowd without nerves, but speaking is a different story. I freeze every time.

"You'll do fine." He shoots me a reassuring smile, and I take a calming breath.

We are the third group to go. Standing in front of the class feels like the longest five minutes of my life, but I survive. Matt doesn't seem nervous at all. He maintains eye contact with the class and talks with smooth, steady intonation. I, on the other hand, say "um" at least a thousand times, lock my eyes on the whiteboard or the floor, and speed through my speech. When we finally finish, I breathe a sigh of relief.

"Good job," Matt whispers on the way back to our seats.

I just roll my eyes. "*You* did good," I whisper back.

Ten

Heather and I meet for coffee on the Friday morning before heading home for Christmas break. It has been snowing for the past couple of days. Everything looks ethereal covered in snow, but it's also treacherous. Just on the way into the coffee shop, I slipped twice. Heather laughed at me before sliding on a patch of ice herself and almost falling.

"Not so funny, huh?" I ask as we walk inside. We order our coffee and take a seat by the window. "How did your final paper go?"

"I'm freaking out. I think I did fine, but part of me feels like I'm going to fail."

"I know! Me too." I take a sip of my latte, the piping hot drink warming me up from the inside.

"But enough about school. We're done!" she cheers before taking a sip of her drink. "What are your plans for the holidays?"

"I have a full house. My grandparents are flying in, and I think my uncle and his family are too, so that will be fun." I raise my eyebrows sarcastically and grin. "You?"

"I'm actually flying out to Oregon to visit my grandparents."

Intrigued, I lean forward. "That sounds fun. Where in Oregon?"

"Corvallis. It's about an hour outside of Salem."

I nod as if I know exactly where that is. "Are you excited?"

"Yeah, I love my grandparents' house, and Oregon is gorgeous. Have you ever been?"

"No. I've only seen pictures." I sigh, imagining the vivid greenery.

"You should come out sometime."

"I'll think about it."

We finish our coffee and agree to text each other over break. Once I get back to the dorms, I finish packing up my last few things and drive home.

The first week of winter break passes quietly. Shelby has school for another week, so during the day, I have the house to myself. It's nice to have alone time, but it's also a little unsettling. Usually during winter break, McKenzie and I would hang out at her house or mine. Most nights, we would huddle by her fire pit making smores and drinking hot chocolate. We'd talk about school, what we wanted for Christmas, what boys we thought were cute. Of course, once Justin entered the picture, it became what boy would be good for Kelsey. This year, I lounge around the house and watch television until Shelby gets home. She does her homework, we eat dinner as a family, and then it's time for bed.

Shelby and I saved our Christmas shopping for the last minute, which was probably a bad idea. Then again, staying home on the days leading up to Christmas isn't much better. Grandparents, aunts, and uncles will be showing up in the next couple of days, and my mom wants to make sure everything is clean, bedrooms set, and not a single speck of dust anywhere. If she spots me on the couch, she gives me a task. It's better to be out on the town.

"There are so many people here," Shelby says, scanning the hordes of last-minute shoppers around the mall. I went shopping for her earlier in the week—having found her some cute hair accessories, a necklace, and a charm bracelet—but now we need presents for our parents.

"Yep. Everyone needs Christmas presents," I say, meeting her gaze. "Where should we start?"

"Let's go look at shoes for Mom."

I take her hand, and we stroll toward the escalator. While we are ascending, Shelby asks about school.

"It wasn't bad," I say with a shrug. "College is college."

"McKenzie always said school was fun. I bet she would have loved college," Shelby says with a smile, and then it slowly fades. She stares down at the floor as we step off the escalator.

"Yeah, she was such a nerd," I tease, smiling. McKenzie's parents never had to tell her to do her homework—she would already be done and wish she had more to do. I always offered mine, but she told me I had to do my own work.

Shelby looks up at me. "A cool nerd," she bubbles, the smile returning to her face.

"The coolest," I respond. Despite the fond memories, my heart still aches just talking about her.

"Do you miss her?" Shelby asks as we enter the shoe store.

"Every single day," I say. *Every day, every hour, every minute.* The thought brings tears to my eyes, so I take a breath and change the subject. "Let's find some shoes."

The store is crowded, shoppers milling around every aisle. I regret wearing a sweater because I am starting to suffocate in this store, the thermostat set to sweltering. I push my sleeves up as high as they go and try not to think about it. Except Shelby and I cannot agree on a pair of shoes, prolonging our stay. And once we finally find a pair, the line for the checkout extends down one shoe aisle and wraps around to the next. By the time we exit, sweat drenches my back. It's a little better out of the store, but the crowds haven't thinned.

"Now for Dad," I say. "What should we get him?"

"Something sports-related? Doesn't he like the Bears?"

My dad was born in Chicago and spent fifteen years there before his family moved to Texas, and then to Arizona. No matter where he lived, his family remained a Bears family. Shelby and I decide to check the sports store. As we head that way, someone calls my name behind me. I turn to see a few of the youth from church. Among them, Justin.

"Hi," I say. The rest keep walking, but Justin stops to talk.

"How are you?" he asks, shifting his weight between his feet.

"I'm doing okay, you?"

"Doing good. Home for the holidays?"

"Yeah," I say, fidgeting with the sleeve of my sweater. We were never great talkers. Any time McKenzie left the two of us alone, this is how conversations would go—short, awkward small talk.

"How's school?" Justin asks, clearing his throat.

"It's okay. How's ASU?" I ask.

"Really good." He nods.

"That's…good." We reach another unbearable pause as neither of us knows what to say. I want to ask him how he is doing without McKenzie, but I don't want to bring that up right now. Not here.

"Well, I guess I should let you two get back to shopping," he says. "Will I see you at Christmas Eve service?"

"Yes. I'm a sheep," Shelby says proudly. She is one of four sheep in the manger scene for the Nativity.

"Right on." Justin holds out his hand for a high five. Shelby slaps his palm, a huge grin on her face. Justin looks at me expectantly, clearly awaiting an answer. I haven't decided if I want to go yet. I know I should, and most likely I will have to because it's the holidays and my family will want to go. Plus, Shelby is a sheep, so it is bound to be cute.

"We'll see," I say. Shelby glances at me, confused.

"I hope you come." Justin pauses, tucking his thumbs in his jean pockets. "Shelby, I look forward to seeing you as a sheep. You are going to rock!" He gives her another high five. "Kels, it was good to see you." I don't know why, but when he says that, I want to cry. He seemed truly happy to see me, relieved even.

"You too," I say. As Shelby and I walk away hand in hand, I contemplate our brief meeting. Justin seems to be doing great, but I wonder how much of it is a façade. How much is he hurting on the inside? Is he really doing that well? He seems to have it more together than I do, and it doesn't even look like he's trying. As for me, I'm constantly trying, constantly putting on a smile so everyone will think I'm fine.

"Here it is," Shelby says, tugging on my hand as we walk. Once we find a jersey for our dad, we head home.

Over the next few days, our house becomes crowded and chaotic as family flies in. First, my aunt and uncle. Then, my grandparents on my mom's side. All the space I had a week ago has vanished, and I feel claustrophobic in my own house. These are the times I would go over to McKenzie's, but now with nowhere to go, I can't escape the crowds.

The day before Christmas Eve, I'm in a sour mood because a lady cut me off on the drive for coffee. When I finally arrived at the coffee shop, the barista made my drink wrong twice before finally getting it right. This hectic time of year has me exhausted. I walk into my overflowing house to Shelby and my two cousins making jewelry in her room. The air mattress I am sleeping on is littered with strings and beads. Annoyed, I turn right back around and head for the front door.

"Hey, there she is," my uncle James says, hustling down the hall.

I give a half-hearted wave, not wanting to stay and make small talk.

"Where are you off to?" he asks.

"Just going out," I say, trying to keep my voice even.

"Out? You just got in. Why don't you stay and visit? Let us know how college life is."

"It's college," I say flatly.

"Come on. Parties, classes, boys, living on your own. That has to be nice."

"Not really," I snap, my aggravation getting the better of me.

"Kelsey," my dad chides from where he can hear us around the corner.

"I'll be home later." My dad says something, but I ignore him. I slam the door on the way out. I start my car and back out of the driveway. There's no destination in mind, but it's like my internal autopilot takes over. Before I know it, I'm in McKenzie's neighborhood and in front of the Fosters' house.

Putting the car in park, I stare at the familiar home for a minute. I glance over at their side gate. During the winter, I often used to enter through there. I hop out of the car and approach the gate, hesitating only a moment before reaching over and pulling the latch up. The latch releases with a familiar click. I step in, remembering this was where I first found out about Justin and McKenzie.

The day was turning out to be brutal. Work was crappy—the customers must have all been wearing cranky pants. No matter what I did, I could not make anyone happy. Then, when I arrived home, Shelby was crying. Turns out, she had a double ear infection. My own ears hurt just from her piercing screams. I had already texted McKenzie about my day at work and told her some backyard time may be needed, as well as chocolate. Shelby put things over the top. When I couldn't take it anymore, I escaped to McKenzie's. With the weather cooling down, we were spending more time in the backyard, so I entered through the gate. I stepped in and was just about to turn the corner when Justin's voice stopped me in my tracks.

"Will it be so bad if she sees me?" Justin asked.

"Yes! She has already had a rough day. I don't want to make her more mad," McKenzie answered.

"You really think she will be mad?"

"No. Well…I don't know, but I don't want to find out."

"McKenzie," Justin pleaded.

"Justin," she said, sounding frustrated.

The voices seemed to be drawing closer, so I took a few steps back.

"You're going to have to tell her eventually," Justin pointed out.

"I will, but not tonight."

"When?" he asked, waiting for an answer. I was just as curious. It was quiet for a few heartbeats. "If you don't, I will."

"No, you won't," she said sternly.

"Yes, actually. I can come with you to her dance competition. It will be perfect."

"Absolutely not."

"Either you tell her, or she finds out when I show up Saturday. Your choice."

They were so close now I could hear their footsteps. Within seconds, they'd be rounding the corner.

"Look, I'll tell her," McKenzie said.

"Tonight?"

"Maybe." I knew that tone. That was a no.

"Saturday, then," he said sternly. The edge of his shoulder came into view. He took another step backward, and I held my breath.

"Justin, look—"

"Saturday," he repeated.

Justin took another step. Two more steps, and he would run into me. McKenzie rounded the corner.

"I'd go with Saturday," I said.

McKenzie's face went white. Justin spun around. "Hey, Kels," he said.

"Justin," I greeted, eyes locked on McKenzie.

"I-I'm going to take off," he said, glancing back at McKenzie. When he turned, he nodded at me and then walked out through the gate. All the while, I didn't break eye contact with McKenzie.

"So, what's going on?" I asked when the gate latched with his exit.

"Nothing," she said, turning and scurrying back toward the fire pit.

"It didn't seem like nothing." I followed her, arms crossed. "It sounded like you two are seeing each other."

"It's only been three dates," she blurted.

"Why didn't you tell me?"

"I wasn't sure it was going to work."

"Why not?"

She shrugged. "We've been friends for a while. What if we went on one date and it was a disaster? I wasn't sure there was anything to report."

"There obviously is." I gestured between her and the gate for emphasis.

"You think?" she asked, a huge grin spreading across her face.

"I know," I said with confidence. "You two have been into each other since the day you met."

"Nah-uh." She shook her head, but her smile gave her away.

"Yah-huh," I retorted.

I stand in the side yard recalling that night. I think about how Justin seemed to be doing okay at the mall the other day, how he seemed sad but not *mad* at the funeral. No one seems angry—or, at least, no one says it. People continue to tell me it's okay to cry, it's okay to be sad, time heals all wounds. But no one has said it's okay to feel angry. The only person to ever bring it up was Matt. And unfortunately, he's also been the recipient of so much of this anger. There at the gate, I break down in tears. I assume I'm alone until someone puts their arms around me and starts to pull me in for an embrace.

"No!" I push away.

"Kelsey, it's okay," Delia assures me.

I step back. "No, no, it's not okay!"

"Sweetie, take a breath. Come talk with me."

"I don't want to talk!" I snap. Fresh tears begin to fall.

Delia takes a step back, giving me space. She doesn't leave though.

"I don't understand," I choke out.

"What do you not understand?" Delia asks, her voice gentle.

"How everyone can still show up to church, still think that God is so wonderful. I'm furious. He took my best friend!"

Delia is silent for a moment. "Kelsey, I *am* angry. I'm angry McKenzie isn't here. I'm angry she isn't in a dorm room, going to classes. I'm angry she isn't here for the holidays. I'm angry I lost my baby. I don't understand why any of this happened, so yes, I am angry, sweetheart. And you have every right to be angry as well."

My mouth drops in shock. "How come no one has said anything?"

"I think it's something we all deal with in our own way."

"You still go to church, though," I point out, slightly accusingly. "I can't even sit through worship without getting angry."

"Trust me, I have had many conversations—some extremely loud—with my Heavenly Father."

"And?" I ask.

"And, God gave me McKenzie for a short time," she says. I start shaking my head. "Kelsey, God gave her to me, and it was her time."

"No!" I shout.

She lets out a heavy breath. "I hate it too, but God has a bigger plan. I don't understand it, but I have to accept it. God called her home. During this time, God has given me comfort and has let me be angry and yell. He has shown me love and mercy. He wants to do the same for you."

I break down again. This time, I let Delia embrace me. I let the hot, angry tears roll down my face. I let the hurt and fury I've been holding in for months escape my body. And through it all, Delia continues to hold me tight.

After my meltdown subsides, I feel better than I have in months. It's cathartic to finally express what I've been feeling. Matt was the first to tell me it was okay to be angry, I just needed to direct my anger toward the right person. Hearing Delia admit that she also harbored anger made me feel a little less alone.

Leaving the Fosters', I pull up to my house, the living room light streaming from the otherwise dark home. It's late. Who would still be up at this time? I crack the door open and tiptoe into the living room, spotting my dad on the couch watching the news. He mutes the television when he sees me, his expression relaxing.

"How was your night?" he asks.

"Not bad. I stopped by the Fosters' place," I tell him.

"How are they?"

"They're…good. It was really nice to catch up."

My dad studies my face. "How are *you*?"

"Better," I say confidently.

"I know you've had a tough time. You know you can talk to your mom and me any time, about anything."

I nod. "It's just been hard to talk." I sit next to him, and he leans over to kiss my cheek. "Sorry about earlier."

He chuckles. "This house is crazy. I don't blame you for not wanting to be here. Sometimes, *I* don't want to be here. Too many people."

I nod in agreement.

"Just remember—they don't get to see you often, so they want to soak up as much time with you as possible before they leave. And so do I." He squeezes me tight, and I can't help but giggle. Once I sober, he says, "I understand taking time for you, if you need it. Just make sure to carve out time for them too."

"I will."

He pats my knee before getting up, handing me the remote.

"Good night, sweetie," he says. "Love you."

"Love you too." I blow him a kiss. Alone on the couch, I lean into the cushions, watching the silent newscaster for a minute. In the right corner is a picture of a Santa who has just been arrested. I think about turning on the volume to find out what Santa did to land him in jail, but my eyelids are already drooping. I turn off the TV and retreat to Shelby's room. My cousins have crashed on the air mattress. Quietly grabbing my pajamas, I get ready for bed. I briefly regret not taking up the Fosters on their offer to stay the night. There, I have a bed. Here, I currently have a couch. I grab a pillow and a blanket out of the hall closet and curl up, falling asleep as soon as I close my eyes. For the first time in months, I sleep peacefully.

Eleven

My mom's face lights up the moment I step downstairs on Christmas Eve. I smile back at her. Stepping into that sanctuary won't be easy, but it is Christmas Eve, and Shelby is a sheep. I can't miss it. I just hope I can make it through the service.

When we get to the church, every pew is packed. My mom takes Shelby to the choir room while the rest of us find our seats. Seeing Delia and John across the aisle, I wave. Delia beams when she sees me. *You can do this*, she mouths. I shoot her a grateful smile. The lights dim, and the band gathers at the front. I take a deep breath.

I can do this.

The service is tolerable, though there are moments that spike my frustration, and the Nativity play is irresistibly cute. Shelby is an excellent sheep, and she's so proud of her performance. After the service, my family heads over to the café for cookies and hot chocolate. I spot Delia and John heading for their car and run to catch up with them.

"Hi," I say.

"Hey, sweetie," Delia says, squeezing me. "Shelby did wonderful."

"Yeah, she did," I say with a chuckle.

"You did too."

"Thanks," I say quietly.

"I remember when you and McKenzie were up there. One wise *woman* and Mary." Delia takes a shaky breath. John reaches over to squeeze her hand. This night must be hard for her too.

"Yeah, I was *not* happy I had to be a wise man," I say to lift the mood. "And you bribed me. You told me if I did it, I would get first pick of the brownies you made." I giggle at the memory.

Delia smiles. "Corner piece, because it had two edges—the best part."

"Always."

A silence falls over us as we relive the bittersweet memory.

"Well, I guess I should let you guys go," I say after a pause.

"It was so good to see you," Delia says. "Feel free to come by tomorrow."

"Are you sure you want me to?" I ask.

"Of course," John says. "It wouldn't be Christmas without seeing you."

When I turn back to Delia, she has tears in her eyes.

"I will," I say, holding back my own tears. I lean in to hug Delia, and she holds me tight. When she pulls away, she wipes her eyes.

I walk back to the cafe with that familiar ache in my chest.

At our house, Christmas morning is off to a running start by 5 a.m. It starts with hushed whispers and overeager voices from Shelby and our cousins, Macy and Olivia. I squeeze my eyes closed, trying to ignore them as they chatter away while waiting for the grown-ups to wake up. When Shelby sees my eyes blink open, she shoots me an apologetic look. I wink at her. Honestly, I am just as excited about presents as she is. She giggles and bounces over to the air mattress.

"Merry Christmas," I whisper to her.

"Merry Christmas," she whispers back. I get up to wrap Macy and Olivia in a hug. As the minutes tick by, the girls grow more impatient. All whispers cease when a door unlatches. We freeze. The door creaks open, and my uncle peeks his head in to check on us.

"You're up!" a chorus greets him. He doesn't look the least bit surprised.

Not long after, we're all packed into the living room. The younger girls open all their presents first before I open mine, and the grown-ups take turns opening presents afterward. Soon, the floor is a sea of wrapping paper and bows. As I watch the girls play with their new toys, I think about the Fosters. It seems like just yesterday that McKenzie and I were that age while Delia and John sat by and watched us open presents and play. This morning can't be easy for them. After getting dressed, I say a quick goodbye to the family before driving to the Fosters' house.

It's still pretty early, I realize as I reach for the doorbell. I hesitate. Maybe it's *too* early. I should have sent a text or something. As I dig through my purse for my phone, the door opens.

"Good morning," John greets me.

"Hi," I say. "Sorry if it's early."

He chuckles. "You were always a morning person on Christmas. Why would this year be any different?" He steps aside to let me in and I follow him to the kitchen.

He pours a cup of coffee and holds up the pot, raising his eyebrows. I accept his nonverbal offer. He grabs a mug out of the cabinet and pours me a cup, and I breathe in the earthy, nutty aroma. I would always show up early on Christmas. Delia isn't one for mornings, so it was usually me, McKenzie, and John. We would start our morning out by the fire pit, coffee in hand. I glance out the back window.

"We can go out there," John says, following my gaze.

"I don't know," I say. This is harder than I expected.

John grabs two packages of Pop-Tarts—another Christmas morning tradition at the Foster house—and unlocks the back door. He starts a fire in the fire pit, then sinks into a lawn chair as I do the same. We relax quietly in the backyard for a moment, just sipping our coffee. He opens a package of Pop-Tarts and offers me one. I take it, and we wordlessly munch on our cold, crumbly pastries.

"How are you guys, really?" I finally ask. "Delia seemed like she was having a rough time last night."

John stares into his coffee. His forlorn expression brings a pang to my chest. "Some days are harder than others. We just take it day by day," he says, not looking up.

"I know," I whisper.

He fixes his eyes on me. "I'm so glad you're here this morning. I miss coffee out here."

I smile. The door slides open and Delia walks out in her pajamas, mug in hand. She sits next to me. This is how Christmas always went. Breakfast outside, presents, and then lunch. Delia would always go all out for lunch. I wonder what she's doing this year.

"Are you joining us for lunch?" she asks as if she read my mind.

"If you want me to."

"You are more than welcome. We have steak, mashed potatoes, glazed carrots, broccoli, and rolls." She winks.

My mouth waters just listening. "Yeah, I can stay."

At first, it's not easy to find a rhythm, but after a while, we're chatting and laughing, each of us bringing up memories and funny stories from past years. Soon, it's just like old times. I help prepare the carrots and the broccoli, like always. No presents are exchanged this year. In fact, I notice their house is lacking in decorations, but I don't ask. This year has been difficult. Day by day, John had said. I guess that's all we can really do.

Matt and Heather text, wishing me a Merry Christmas, and I respond to each. Matt lives down in the valley as well, and since we have a couple of weeks before school starts again, I ask if he'd like to meet for coffee sometime. Of all people, I've learned, he'd be the one to understand how I'm feeling right now. He agrees, and we schedule our meetup.

Matt is seated at one of the metal tables outside of Starbucks when he spots me.

"Hey, how goes it?" he asks with a wave.

"Pretty good," I say. He gets up and holds the door open for me. We order our coffee and pick up our drinks before heading back outside.

"So, I went to McKenzie's parents' house on Christmas," I begin.

"How was that?" he asks, taking a sip of his coffee.

"Good, I think…I don't know. I hate watching them feel sad."

"I get that. How are you?" he asks.

"Well, I had a huge meltdown in their side yard the night before Christmas Eve. But it was actually good to just let myself be sad and angry for once."

He nods, listening attentively.

"Delia, McKenzie's mom, said she was angry too. It made me feel like I wasn't the only one, finally."

Matt dips his head. "No one may know exactly what you're feeling, but people can relate. When I lost my brother, I felt like no one understood. I didn't talk about it because I didn't want to make my parents sad, but all it did was make me angry, which Jake got the brunt of. We stopped talking for a while, even. When I started getting into trouble at school, my parents sat me down to talk. I had been holding in the hurt, the sadness, and the anger for so long, I broke down. My mom looked me right in the eye and told me I could come to her or my dad to talk about Brent any time. After that, I talked with them regularly. I also saw a counselor."

"Did it help?" I ask.

The corner of his lips lifts in a smile. "It did."

I nod, focusing on my coffee and absently swirling my drink with my straw.

"What's up?" he asks.

I glance up quickly and shake my head. "Nothing."

"It's not nothing." He waits for me to speak.

"I was just wondering how you—how anyone—could keep going to church."

He is quiet for a long moment, his brows furrowed in thought.

"You don't have to say anything," I say.

"I was just trying to figure out how to put it. I think it depends on the person." He draws a breath, and I wait as he thinks it through. "I didn't stop going to church, but I stopped praying for a while. It was my way of letting God know I was mad."

"What changed?"

"Just one particular sermon. It was right in the middle of my angry phase; Jake and I had just had a huge argument, and our pastor was talking about forgiveness. I don't recall what verse it was, but at the time it hit me like a ton of bricks. I realized then I was being a jerk. This was right before I talked with my parents about everything. After that, I started praying again, little prayers at first. But then I really started praying and reading my Bible."

I just sit there, mesmerized by his story.

Matt chuckles. "Doesn't help, does it?"

"No, it does."

He continues, "I think a good first step for you is to talk. It sounds like McKenzie's parents are here for you and want to hear from you. You have your parents too. And you can also talk to me. If it's too hard, though, a counselor is a good way to go. They're not directly involved, so it's easier to open up about some things."

"Thanks." I smile at him.

He gives me a sympathetic look. "Honestly, it just takes time. God will be ready whenever you are."

I breathe deeply to gather myself before meeting his gaze. "I get it." I wipe at my eyes and Matt changes the subject to upcoming classes and what we did on our Christmas breaks.

Before I know it, Christmas break is over, and school is starting up again. Returning to campus brings up mixed feelings. I'm happy to be in my dorm room again, but I miss my family. Overall, I'm excited to see my friends—to see Matt.

The first day back from break, McKenna is surprisingly polite.

"Hey," she says, popping her earbuds out when I step into the room.

"Hi," I say as I set down my duffel bag.

"How was your holiday?" she asks.

I stare back at her for a moment, confused. "Uh, good," I finally say. "Yours?"

"It was good. Really enjoyed not having any homework."

"Me too." I turn my attention to my phone, marveling at how many words we've just exchanged. This is the longest conversation we've had since my big party blunder.

"So…" She pauses, and I look up. "I'm sorry for being such a jerk at the beginning of the year."

The apology catches me off guard.

"Don't get me wrong, I think you were a complete jerk too, but at least you owned up to it and apologized."

"You're…welcome?" I have no idea what to say.

"So this is me owning up to my…jerkiness. I'm sorry. I don't really want to spend the rest of the year hating you."

"Apology accepted. I am sorry again for the party and—"

She holds up her hand. "Let's just move on. We don't have to be friends or anything, but we can be good acquaintances."

"Okay." I smile at her. She grins back before putting her earbuds in again, a peaceful agreement reached.

I hope it can stay this way.

Twelve

A new semester means new classes. I walk into my astronomy class and take a seat at one of the black laminate tables. Up front, three whiteboards stand side by side. A model of the solar system hangs from the ceiling.

"Is this taken?" Matt asks, grabbing the empty seat next to me.

I jump at his sudden approach. "What are *you* doing here?"

"I'm in this class." He pulls out the class textbook and a notebook.

"Coincidence?" I ask, raising an eyebrow.

He looks at me with an unreadable expression. "Totally."

The professor walks in, checks his watch, and turns to the whiteboard. He writes the course number and his name down, then passes out the syllabus.

The professor scans the room with a stern expression, crossing his arms. "You are not going to want to miss a single class. If you do, be sure you have an excellent partner who can catch you up."

Matt and I glance at each other. *Wow*, I mouth.

I'll need an excellent partner, indeed. A couple weeks after classes begin, I wake up with a headache and a sore throat. I figure I can power through the day, but by the time I get to astronomy class, I am beat. Matt hasn't arrived yet, so I lay my head on the black laminate table, which feels nice and cool against my skin. Could I be running a temperature? Footsteps approach the table, but I don't open my eyes to see who it is.

"Hey," Matt says. I blink my eyes open and slowly lift my head. His eyes widen when he sees my face. "Woah, you look awful."

"Gee, thanks." I wince as the words come out. My throat feels like sandpaper.

He doesn't hesitate. "Come on, let's go." He holds out his hand.

"Go? Class is about to start," I whisper, which does nothing to ease the pain.

"Yeah. You don't need to be here, though."

I take his hand and let him pull me up.

"Holy cow," he says, placing his free hand on my forehead. It feels so cool on my skin. "Come on." He grabs my backpack and leads me out of class. When we are just outside the door, I stop.

"Are you okay?" he asks, looking concerned.

"One of us needs to stay here," I say, biting my lip to keep from crying.

"I'm not leaving you," he says adamantly, but I hold my ground.

"I'll be fine," I protest. "Go to class, take notes."

He scrutinizes my face. Finally, he hands me my backpack, which suddenly weighs a thousand pounds. I don't compensate for the weight quick enough and almost drop it. Matt reaches out. He doesn't drop his hands until my backpack is securely in place.

"Text me as soon as you get to your dorm," he says, voice laced with worry.

I don't even try to talk—I just nod. I hobble toward the doors at the end of the hall. When I reach the door, I glance back. Matt still stands at the end of the hall, watching me, then waves and heads into class. My phone chimes a few moments later.

As soon as you are in your dorm! Matt's text reads.

I somehow drag myself back to my room, my body aching with each step. I drop my backpack by my bed and collapse on the mattress. I roll over and type a quick text to Matt before kicking off my shoes and falling asleep.

The sun has already gone down when I wake up. My head feels a little better, but my throat is still on fire. I glance at my phone to check the time, but when I unlock the screen, my phone floods with messages.

Did you make it back?

Kelsey? Are you okay?

You promised. Text me back.

Did you make it to your dorm?

Kelsey Lanter, are you alive?

The message I sent Matt before passing out is still waiting in the text box. I never actually sent it. Poor Matt has been freaking out. I am about to respond when I hear a knock on my door. I fight to my feet— everything still hurting—and open the door.

"Hey," Matt says, seemingly breathing out a sigh of relief.

"Sorry," I croak. "My message didn't send."

"At least you're okay. I brought some supplies." He holds up a small brown paper bag as proof.

I step aside to let him in and shuffle back over to my bed, huddling under the covers, as he displays the pharmacy he bought on my desk.

"We have throat lozenges, cough syrup, Tylenol, ramen noodles, and Sprite." He wheels around to face me, and I can't help but smile.

"Do you need anything else?" he asks. I shake my head. He walks over, placing his hand gingerly on my forehead. "You're burning up." He grabs the box of Tylenol and hands it to me. "Take this."

I take the medication and start to get up.

"Woah, woah. What are you doing?" he asks.

"Getting water," I whisper. He shakes his head and walks over to the fridge, grabs a bottle of water, and brings it back to me. "Thanks."

"You're welcome. Get some rest, and I'll check on you later," he says. Once he sees himself out, I take the Tylenol, change into pajamas, and hide under my comforter.

A coughing fit rouses me from my shallow sleep. I crawl out of bed with a groan to grab the throat lozenges and cough syrup Matt brought. McKenna rouses and rolls over, her eyes on me as I shuffle to my desk.

"You okay?" she whispers.

I shake my head.

"Do you need anything?"

Again, I shake my head. I grab the bottle of cough syrup and the lozenges before making the journey back to my bed. Once McKenna sees me sink into my mattress, she rolls back over. It takes about twenty minutes for the medicine to kick in, and I drift into a fitful sleep. The next time I wake up, the sun is shining, and McKenna is gone.

I slept through my first class, but if I get up now, I can catch my next two classes and dance rehearsal. I take a dose of cough syrup before leaving and grab the bag of lozenges. When I arrive at rehearsal, I regret not grabbing the bottle of Tylenol. Every muscle aches and the cough syrup has worn off. I set my bag down and start to change my shoes when a coughing fit erupts from my chest. Several of the girls grab their stuff and move away from me, and Ms. Oliver casts me a worried glance. Once she finishes her conversation, she strides over to me.

"Hey, Kelsey. That does not sound good."

"It doesn't feel great," I rasp.

"Are you sure you want to participate today? Would you rather go home?"

"We have the competition coming up," I point out.

"That's true, and while I admire your dedication, I would rather you go home and get better if you're sick. The decision is ultimately yours, but just know I won't be upset if you choose to go home."

"I'll at least watch for a bit."

Ms. Oliver nods and starts rehearsal. I start to doze off about halfway through the routine. When Ms. Oliver prods me awake, I'm lying on the floor. "Kels, I think it's best if you go home."

I nod and pack up my stuff, hearing a chorus of "feel better" as I trudge out the door.

When I step into my building, someone calls my name.

"What are you doing out of bed?" Heather chides, marching toward me.

"Heather, she's not in her room," Matt calls from the stairs. When he sees me, his brow instantly furrows. He rushes toward us. "Where were you?"

"I had rehearsal."

"You went to rehearsal?" Heather sounds shocked.

I nod. My legs are about to give out, and my dance bag seems to weigh a ton. Even though I'm wearing a sweater and a winter jacket, I feel chilled and begin to shiver. Once again, Matt places a hand on my forehead.

"Jeez." He takes my bag, gesturing for me to lead. "Let's get you to bed."

When I finally make it to my door, I lean against the wall to catch my breath. That was way harder than it should have been.

Matt shakes his head. "I can't believe you went to rehearsal."

"I"—*wheeze*—"had to"—*wheeze*—"be there." I reach for my gym bag, and Matt holds it out to me. I find my keys in the side pocket and open the door.

As the door swings open, I start hacking again.

"Woah, that sounds awful."

"It feels awful," I say, my eyes watering.

We step inside, and Matt sets my bag down. I kick off my boots, slip off my jacket, and immediately crawl under my covers.

"Can I get you anything?"

"I'll probably make some ramen in a minute," I whisper.

"Allow me," Matt offers.

I direct him on where to find a bowl, and he microwaves the noodles. He brings the bowl over along with a bottle of water. I sit there, stirring the noodles without eating them.

"Not hungry?" he asks. I shrug. I thought I was, but now that the noodles are in front of me, I don't feel hungry.

"Can I get you something else?"

I shake my head and yawn, wincing when the movement brings a stab of pain. I suck in a breath, which catches in my dry throat and kickstarts my coughing—the deep, barking kind.

Matt raises an eyebrow. "Have you taken any cough syrup?"

"Yes," I rasp. "It works pretty good." I grab the bottle from my nightstand, twist the cap off, and pour myself another dose. I down it quickly, wrinkling my nose at the flavor.

"Doesn't taste good, though," he comments.

I shake my head.

"Sorry," he says with a sympathetic smile. "I think I'll let you get some rest." He walks over to press his hand to my forehead, which is starting to feel like a routine.

"I'm so hot," I tease.

"You are." He winks at me as he drops his hand. My stomach somersaults, and while I could blame it on the sickness, I know it's not. I know exactly what this is.

He ambles over to the door and calls out, "Get some rest" before closing it behind him. I pick at my noodles, eating a couple of bites before giving up and lying back down. McKenna doesn't come back to the room, and just after curfew, my phone chimes.

Hey! Not coming back to the room. How are you feeling? McKenna's text reads.

I'm exhausted. Sorry for kicking you out, I respond.

Don't worry about it. I hope you feel better.

Thanks.

I stow my phone and stare up at the ceiling, wondering when this miserable ordeal will end.

Thirteen

When I wake up Wednesday, I take a dose of cough medicine and some Tylenol. I have to make it through two classes and a session in the gym tonight. On the way out, I hesitate and then grab the bottle of Tylenol. Matt is already seated at our table in astronomy. He looks shocked to see me.

"Hey," I greet him as I take my seat.

"Hi. How are you?"

"Well, I'm here," I say.

"You are." I notice a little crease appear on his forehead.

"I'm fine," I reassure him as I start to cough. A few students in front of me glance back, giving me the evil eye. Oops. Luckily, the professor walks in and commands everyone's attention.

During the lecture, I begin to nod off when I feel Matt nudge my elbow. I wiggle in my chair in an attempt to wake myself up. Halfway through class, my head starts to pound. Great. We still have astronomy lab to get through, and I have a group workout.

"Are you going to make it through lab?" Matt asks as we pack up.

"I'll just get a coffee and power through." I smile at him, but he doesn't return it.

After class, we head straight for the coffee shop. The bright sunlight aggravates my headache as I try to squint against the glare. I pull open the door to a bustling student crowd. A loud crash from behind the counter makes me flinch. Matt leans down and whispers in my ear, "Vanilla latte?"

I nod vigorously, surprised he remembered my favorite drink.

"Wait out here. I got it."

Matt steps around me and heads to the counter. Worn out, I sit on the bench outside, propping my elbows on my knees and resting my head in my palms.

"Here you go." I lift my head and Matt extends a steaming drink toward me. Once I take it, he holds out his hand. I accept it and let him help me up. I assume he'll let go once I'm up, but instead, he starts walking with our hands still clasped. I could let go, but I don't. It feels good, like two puzzle pieces fitting together perfectly.

Lab begins with little fanfare. I pop two Tylenol capsules, washing them down with a sip of my latte. Matt furiously takes notes, which I should be doing, but I can hardly keep my head off the desk. In our short break, Matt rubs my back in little, concentric circles. My whole body tingles at his touch. He peeks over at me, and I give him a weak smile.

Once class is over, Matt remarks, "You made it."

"Barely."

"Yeah, but now you can rest."

I shake my head. "We have to be at the gym tonight," I say with a grimace.

"Kels, you look exhausted. The harder you push yourself, the longer this is going to take to clear up," Matt chides, visibly agitated. "I'm sure the team will understand."

"We have a game Saturday and the competition next week. I can't miss gym or rehearsals right now."

"You're impossible," he complains, taking my hand again. My attention narrows to his touch. "Can you at least nap before tonight?"

"I can, but I wasn't planning on it. I have five classes to keep up with."

"Do you want to go over what you missed earlier this week?"

"Yes please."

Matt shakes his head in disapproval but leads me back to his dorm. An hour later, hunched over Matt's desk, I've copied half of the notes from Monday. My eyelids are heavy, and keeping them open takes effort. Finally, I give up and lay my head down.

"I have a bed."

"I'm not sleepy," I mumble.

I hear the door open. "Hey," Jake whispers. "Is she…?"

"She's not sleeping," Matt answers.

I sit up. "I'm totally awake."

Matt shakes his head at me. "How's Heather?"

That catches my attention. "What's wrong with Heather?" I ask.

"She caught whatever this is." He waves his hand in my general direction.

I cringe. "Oh no! I hope she feels better soon."

"Me too. I hate to see her so miserable," Jake says. From his pitiful expression, I can tell it really does hurt him to see her sick. It's kind of romantic. "I'm just grabbing some supplies, and then I'm going to go take care of my girl."

"I should probably get going too," I say to Matt.

"I'll walk you there." Matt grabs my dance bag and once we're out of the room, he extends his hand to me. I reach out and, this time, Matt laces his fingers in mine. Matt is kind enough to walk with me at my pace. We stop once for me to cough and catch my breath. That little crease appears on Matt's forehead again. When I stop at the parking lot, Matt frowns.

"Kels, are you sure going to the gym is a good idea?"

"Yep." I flash a smile. "I just need to be there. I won't push it."

Matt shakes his head. "All right."

I turn to him and reach for my bag. Matt seems reluctant to hand it over, like if he holds it hostage, I won't be able to go. After a moment, he slips the strap off his shoulder and hands it over. He doesn't fully release it until he's sure I have a good hold on it.

"I'll be okay." I try reassuring him. "I'll text you later?"

"Sure," he says, but the look of concern still lingers.

Matt releases my hand and instantly I wish I didn't have to let go. I begin across the parking lot, looking back a couple times. Matt stands on the curb, watching me. I give a small wave when I reach my car and then climb in.

On the way to the gym, I think about the walk from the coffee shop to his dorm and just now, his hand in mine. It was so comforting, so natural. Who am I fooling? I know I like him, and it seems like he likes me.

I wonder what McKenzie would say if she were here. Would it be a "duh" moment, like clearly this is going to be a thing, like it was with her and Justin? Or would she be totally against it, insisting on being the only photographer in my life? From there, my thoughts dive deeper. If McKenzie were here, would Matt and I have ever met, ever become friends? If McKenzie and I had our way, we would have been photography partners. And I would have never worked with Matt.

Days of ramen have left me craving anything else. I'm heading toward the dining hall when I hear my name. I look around and spot Matt jogging toward me.

"Where are you headed?" His eyes flick to my dance bag and his jaw tightens.

"Grabbing food." I see his tension begin to melt until I add, "Then heading to rehearsal."

He sighs. "Want company?"

I lift my shoulder. "If you want."

Matt slides his hand into mine and we make our way to the dining hall.

Inside, I sit at the first table available and drop my gym bag. I let out a groan when I see the long, snaking line to the counter.

"I can bring you food. What sounds good?"

"A grilled cheese," I answer.

Matt returns to the table carrying a plate full of meatloaf, potatoes, and salad. The second plate is sparse. He takes a seat across from me and slides the nearly empty plate over to me.

The lingering congestion makes it hard to breathe, so chewing with my mouth closed is nearly impossible. After a few bites, I set my sandwich down.

Matt pauses mid-bite. "Everything all right?"

I nod and pick up the grilled cheese, taking a tiny bite.

"You don't have to eat it."

"I'm starving though." I take another small bite, breathing deeply before the next.

Matt studies me for a moment before scooping his potatoes onto my plate. "Try that instead."

"No, I'm fi—" I pause when he lifts an eyebrow at me and points to the potatoes with his fork. I oblige and try a small spoonful. Immediately, the butter melts on my tongue, making it easier to eat.

I shove another scoop into my mouth. "Never mind, this was a good call."

Matt stares at me.

"What? Do I have something on my chin?"

Matt shakes his head. He picks up his fork and takes a bite of his meatloaf. I watch as he does.

Swallowing, he asks, "Are we just going to watch each other eat?"

I chuckle. "No, that would be weird."

He smiles. "Agreed."

After we finish our meal, Matt grabs my gym bag and our tray. He discards our trash in a bin by the exit. As soon as his hands are free I reach over and lace my fingers through his. I glance up and catch him grin.

All sense of happiness fades when we reach my car. Matt inhales. "Kels…"

I don't let him finish his thought. "I'm fine."

He takes a deep breath, releasing it slowly as he deposits my bag in the back seat.

"Take it easy, okay?"

I give his hand a gentle squeeze. "I will."

Before the game on Saturday, I take every medication imaginable. After the routine, cheers erupt from the crowd. I hear a loud whistle and then my name. When I scan the crowd, I catch Matt, Jake, and

Heather in the stands. I give them a small wave and head back to the bench. Our routine is flawless, which makes Ms. Oliver proud. The competition is next week after all, and Ms. Oliver has been striving for perfection.

After the game, the trio find me. I wave as the cold air tickles my lungs, and I start to cough. Jake scans the ground as if searching for something. "No lung," he says when they reach me. "I guess it's still in there, for now."

"Ha ha," I say with a smirk.

"You guys were great out there," Jake says with a big smile.

"Thanks. I think we did pretty good."

"Pretty good?" Matt scoffs. "I would say you killed it."

I smile at him. "Our coach was happy. This routine was by far our best performance yet."

"Want to celebrate with some food, if you're feeling up to it?" Matt asks.

"Sure."

We all ride over to Salsa Brava together, where we're seated at a booth. Matt lets me slide in first.

"How are you, Heather?" I ask.

"Doing good." She smiles. Other than the slight congestion, she sounds like herself. "I've got notes from English 102 for you."

"And I've got some for you. We can work through the material when you feel better," I say with a smile.

During our conversation, I can feel Matt staring at me. I turn to him. "What?"

"How are *you* feeling?" The little crease in Matt's forehead appears again. Over this week, I've come to know it very well.

I shrug. The bucketload of medication I took this morning is wearing off. By the time our waiter comes to take our order, I'm propping myself up with my elbows.

While waiting for our food, Matt places his hand on my knee and gives it a little squeeze. I glance over, shooting him a smile. His hand lingers there until our food comes. I only take a few bites before pushing my plate away.

"You're full?" Jake asks.

"Just not hungry." I shrug, trying to stifle a yawn.

"How did you get over this so fast?" Matt asks Heather.

"I basically did nothing for a few days. Just slept."

"Sounds like what you should've been doing," Matt pointedly says to me. I scrunch my nose at him.

When everyone is finished eating, we head out. Jake drops me and Matt off at his truck. Matt gives me a ride over to my car, pulling into the parking space next to mine. Before I get out, he places a hand on my forehead. After a moment, he shakes his head.

"So, do you not like doctors or something?" he asks.

"Doctors are fine." I glance over at him, wondering what he's getting at.

"If they are fine then why—"

"Because I'm okay," I say.

"I'll admit you seem better than earlier this week," he says as I start coughing. "But not completely better—case in point." He sighs. "If this isn't gone by next week, I'm dragging you in."

"I'd love to see you try."

"You're not that hard to pick up. It'll be a piece of cake."

I snort. "It's not a big deal. I'll be fine."

"It feels like you have a fever again." He gestures to my forehead and fixes me with a hard stare. "I told you not to push yourself."

"What am I supposed to do? I had a game; we have a competition coming up. Not to mention I have classes."

"I'm sure your teachers would understand. Maybe it would be good for you to skip a few classes. Get some real rest."

"Matt," I huff. "I can't skip class."

"Why not?"

"I'm already going to miss classes next week because of our competition."

"So, take a few days and recoup. Isn't it better to be completely healthy before competition anyway?"

I purse my lips and shake my head. "It's not that simple."

"Who says?"

"I do." My voice gains volume.

Matt takes a steadying breath. "I don't get it."

"I know you don't." I suck in a breath, the air catching in my throat causing me to cough again. Matt reaches over and rubs my back. When I'm able to catch my breath, I turn. His hand slips from my back and rests on my side.

"I almost screwed everything up last semester. I don't want to miss too many classes or fall too far behind. I *cannot* miss class."

"I can't speak for the rest of your classes, but you have an outstanding astronomy partner," he boasts and shoots me a goofy smile. "So you don't have to worry about falling behind in that class."

"I appreciate that." I give him a slight grin. "I'll try and rest as much as possible. I just…"

"You need to be in class," he states quietly.

I nod and glance up, seeing genuine care in his eyes.

"I'll take it easy," I say to make him feel better. "Please don't worry."

Matt sighs. "I'll try not to."

We say good night and I head back to my dorm. When I open the door, the lights are off, and McKenna is fast asleep, which is odd because it's just after seven. I check my temperature, and sure enough, I'm running a low-grade fever. I take some Tylenol and pull out my French homework. I'm almost done with one of my past-due assignments when McKenna wakes up coughing.

"Oh no. You caught it?"

She nods.

"There's cough syrup and lozenges on my desk. Help yourself."

"Thanks," she rasps. She takes some cough syrup and lies back down.

On Sunday, I give her the room and head to Starbucks to study. In between my assignments from jazz history, a group of preteen girls strut in, giggling. Their conversation is loud, so I can't help but overhear. One of them has a huge crush on a boy from school. The rest of her friends tell her she needs to ask him out, listing off several ways to start a conversation or get him to notice her. I smile as I turn my attention back to my computer. I remember when McKenzie and I were first allowed to go to the mall or hang out at Starbucks by ourselves. We felt so grown up. We'd talk about school, makeup, and boys while sipping on our Frappuccinos. The memory brings with it a bitter ache. I miss her so much.

"Earth to Kelsey," Matt says, pulling me out of the memory. "This is resting?"

"Hey," I say, clearing my throat.

"What's wrong?" he asks, suddenly looking concerned.

"Nothing."

"Homework got you all choked up?" he teases.

"No. What are you doing here?" I ask to change the subject.

"I needed caffeine, and I *cannot* be in my room anymore."

"Why?" I ask as Matt sits across from me. He fakes sniffling and coughing, then ends his performance by starting to hock a loogie.

"Ew, please stop," I say as several people give us weird looks.

"He has caught the bug," Matt announces dramatically.

"Oh no."

"Tell me about it. After dinner last night he complained of a headache, and this morning, he looked like death."

"That sucks. How are you feeling?"

"I'm feeling okay."

The girls giggle next to us, and I glance over at them. Matt follows my gaze.

"Is everything okay with you?" he asks.

"Yep. Just doing homework," I tell him, trying to sound casual.

"If you want, we can go over astronomy notes," he suggests. As we work, I keep glancing over at the girls, watching as they get up and walk out.

"Kels, what's up?" Matt asks.

"Nothing," I say, trying to focus on the notes.

"You're a sucky liar," he states.

"Don't worry about it." I don't really want to cry in the middle of Starbucks. The truth is, McKenzie's birthday is fast approaching, and I've been thinking about her more often than usual. Watching the girls today makes me miss her even more. I swallow hard, looking up to see Matt's eyes on me.

"You can talk to me."

"I know." I smile at him. He doesn't press.

Once I have all the astronomy notes I missed, we pack up. "You headed back to your room?" I ask him.

"I guess. I really don't want to. He is such a baby when he's sick," Matt complains.

"Most men are."

"Hey, not me," he says defensively.

"Sure you're not." I roll my eyes.

He lightly punches my arm. "I'm not."

On my way out, I pick up a hot green tea with steamed lemonade for McKenna. When I get back to the room, McKenna is sitting in bed with her headphones in.

"Hey, how ya doing?" I ask.

"I'm not dead," she says, still sounding congested.

"You look better. Here." I extend the tea.

She takes it and gingerly takes a sip. "Thanks. This is good." She smiles. I am so relieved our acquaintanceship is still going well.

Fourteen

Matt—the lucky duck—misses the flu bug. After a few grueling weeks, the rest of us are finally better. Heather and I are at lunch when her phone rings.

She picks up, listening to someone on the other end. "What happened?" she asks, her voice raising an octave. My head shoots up. She bends to pick up her purse. "What hospital?" She stumbles up from the table and bolts for the exit.

Hospital? I grab my purse, leaving a few bucks on the table to cover our drinks, and follow her.

"Okay, we'll be there in a minute." There's a pause. "Yes, she's with me." Another pause. "Love you," she says, and then hangs up.

"Who was that?" I ask.

"Jake," she answers, already climbing into her car. I get in and close my door.

"What happened? Is he all right?"

"Someone ran a stop sign and hit Jake's car on the passenger side. He's not badly hurt but went to get checked out."

Seeing her tight lips and scrunched eyebrows, I can tell there's more. "What else?" I ask. She glances over at me.

"Matt was with him," she says carefully, focusing on the road.

Adrenaline surges through me, a sense of dread creeping into the pit of my stomach. I try not to vomit on the spot. "I-is he okay?" I ask, checking my phone for messages from Matt.

"Jake says he's okay—a little more banged up than him."

"What does that mean?" I ask, panic rising to my chest.

"I don't know, but we're about to find out," Heather says, pulling into the hospital parking lot. She finds a spot and hops out, but leans back in when I stay frozen in my seat. "You coming?"

I don't know if I can walk in there. A flashback to the night of McKenzie's accident plays over in my mind. The police, the shattered glass, the blood and her swollen face…

"Kelsey, come on. I'm sure they're fine," Heather says, trying to sound positive. I get out and meet her at the back of the car. She looks so calm. I'm a little jealous.

As we start walking, she grabs my hand. "Totally fine," she whispers to herself, squeezing my hand. She may look calm on the surface, but there must be more going on inside than she is letting on. I squeeze her hand back reassuringly.

When we step inside, only a few seats in the waiting area are occupied. We start to walk over to the admission desk and the clerk, in bright pink scrubs and a slightly disheveled top knot, stands with a look of worry on her face. Heather opens her mouth when someone calls her name. Jake is walking toward us from down the hall. She releases my hand and runs over to him.

"Jake!" she exclaims, pulling him into a tight embrace. He winces but doesn't pull away, hugging her back. She lets him go to step back and look him over. "Seems like you're in one piece."

"Yeah. Couple bruises, but I'm good," he tells her. I shuffle over to them, my feet dragging on the squeaky floor.

"Hi, Jake," I say. "Are you okay?"

"Oh, never better." He chuckles but stops and holds his chest.

"How's Matt?" I ask, my voice shaky.

He purses his lips, and his silence worries me more. "Come on," he says softly. Jake turns, taking Heather's hand and leading us toward another room. He reaches for the door handle and walks in.

"Hey, Heather," I hear Matt say. I pause just outside the threshold, inhaling a trembling breath.

This is just the emergency room, not the ICU. He's awake and talking, which is a good sign, I tell myself. I step into the doorway.

"Hey," Matt says, studying my face.

"Hi," I say, trying to smile. "How are you?"

"I'm all right." He keeps his eyes fixed on my face. Meanwhile, I look him over. His right arm is wrapped up, and a couple of bloodied scrapes mar his right cheek. I take another deep breath when I hear someone coming up behind me. I step into the room to avoid blocking the doorway, letting the nurse in.

"Hey, hon. How's the pain?" she asks Matt, who hasn't torn his eyes from me. I bite my lip.

"Manageable," he says. The nurse shakes her head and points to the scale on the little whiteboard. It starts with a happy face and the number one. The tenth face has tears. "Six," Matt answers. I wonder if he's being honest.

"Okay, then. If you need something for the pain, just let us know. I'll be back in a few minutes to take you for X-rays." She steps out and my heart plummets to the floor.

"Snacks?" Jake asks, receiving a weighted look from Heather. They seem to have a silent conversation before she stands.

"Uh, yeah, snacks. Sounds good." She takes his hand and follows him out of the room.

Once they're gone, Matt turns to me. "Kelsey?" he asks, his voice laced with worry.

"Huh?" I say, my gaze fixed on the polished concrete floor.

"Can you tell me how you're feeling right now?"

"I'm…fine," I say, my voice breaking.

"Kels?"

"I'm fine," I repeat, finally looking up at him. I try to keep my face calm, but I can feel the tears already gathering in my eyes. A flash of McKenzie invades my thoughts—all those tubes, her eye swollen shut. I blink hard.

"You can talk to me. What's going on in that head of yours?"

"It… I…" I can't finish the sentence.

"Can you come here?"

I walk over slowly, one shaky step at a time. When I get to the side of the bed, he takes my hand, squeezing it. I look into his brown eyes and feel a tear roll down my cheek.

"I swear, I'm okay," he says with conviction.

"I believe you," I whisper. Just then, the door opens. I quickly wipe my cheeks and force myself to breathe.

"Ready for X-rays?" the nurse asks. Matt squeezes my hand one more time before releasing it. I step back, and the nurse presses a peddle to release the wheels on the bed. She and an assistant wheel him out the door. I step into the hall to watch them.

"Smile pretty," I call. His short chuckle echoes through the hall.

Now standing here alone, my heart starts to pound. It feels like the walls are closing in around me, and my chest tightens until my breath becomes shallow and raspy. I need to get out, do something.

I rush back toward the emergency waiting room. The phone at the desk rings, unattended, as the admissions clerk argues with a woman about the long wait she's had. Overhead, an announcement plays, but I can't make it out. I meander down a hallway that leads to the main entrance, the gift shop, and a chapel. The last one makes my stomach tighten. I look around for a bathroom, spotting one near the gift shop. I dash to the first open stall and throw up bile. Suddenly, I'm thankful Heather and I didn't have the chance to eat.

When I stand, my vision blurs, then comes back into focus. I stumble over to the sink, my hands shaky as I turn on the faucet. I splash some water on my face and focus on my breathing. My stomach still feels queasy as I wander back to Matt's room.

I hear my three friends chatting as I reach the door. Drawing a steadying breath, I remind myself that Matt is one of the voices. He is okay.

When I step inside, Heather's eyes widen. "Woah, what happened to you?"

"Nothing." My voice is shaky. I force a smile. "So, what'd they say about your arm?"

"It's a nice, clean break," Matt answers.

"Those heal faster." I clear my throat.

"That's what the tech said," Matt says, scrutinizing me.

I shuffle my feet, Jake and Heather having claimed the only two chairs in the room. Matt pats the side of the bed and I take a seat next to him. The same nurse that took him for X-rays pops back in. "We are getting all the paperwork finalized. We'll get a cast put on and—" She glances over at me. "Oh honey, do you need to be checked out?"

"Huh? No?" I stare at her, confused.

"Sometimes if we're in shock, we may not realize we're hurt right away," she begins to explain.

"Oh, no, I wasn't in the accident," I say.

Matt laces his fingers through mine. "She's okay. Just not a fan of hospitals."

The nurse nods at Matt's explanation. "All right. Well, give us a little bit longer and we will get you out of here as soon as possible."

The sun is setting as we walk out, Matt sporting his bright, caution-orange cast. I could tell he was in pain in the hospital, but he refused any pain medication. Now, he winces with every step. I offer my hand to help him down the curb. He takes it, and doesn't let it go.

Jake and Heather are in front and beat us to the car. As we approach, Heather notices our hands intertwined and smiles, raising a quizzical eyebrow at me. I shrug. "I'll need details later," she whispers before we get in.

"Is anyone else hungry?" Jake asks as Heather backs out.

"I'm starving," Heather says.

"I could eat," Matt replies.

"Lou Mings?" I suggest, my stomach having finally calmed down.

"Yes," Jake says with a fist pump and calls to place an order.

A wave of panic creeps up on me as we drive. I close my eyes and breathe. Feeling pressure on my knee, I glance down to see Matt's hand there. I take his hand, interlacing my fingers with his and holding tight. *He is fine. His hand is in yours. He's sitting right next to you. He's okay. You're okay.* I repeat this line of thought like a mantra.

When I feel Matt's hand relax, I peek over to see his head lolled back and his eyes closed. He starts snoring softly. Once we park, Jake and Heather run in to grab the food while I wait in the car with Matt. He finally stirs when Heather pulls into the dorm parking lot.

"Ow." He sits up and rubs his neck.

"How are you holding up?" I ask.

"I feel like I got hit by a car," he says. I grimace.

"Wonder why?" Heather winks at him in the rearview mirror.

"Really, though. Are you okay?" A deep concern for him rests like lead in my stomach.

"Yeah. I'll take something when we get inside," he says.

"The prescriptions!" I exclaim, and everyone looks at me. "We forgot to fill them."

"It's all good. I really want to go inside."

"I'll go get them after dinner," I say.

We all pile out and head for the boys' dorm. Matt walks slowly, like every step hurts. I want to scold him for not taking anything at the hospital.

"Jeez, how far away did you park?" Matt asks Heather.

"I looked for the closest spot," she answers calmly.

"Try harder next time," Matt snaps.

"Sorry…"

Matt stops walking. I stand beside him, waiting for him to continue. "Just a bit farther," I encourage. When Matt does start again, he is shaky. I nestle in closer to his side. "Here." I take his good arm and wrap it around my shoulders, grabbing his waist to steady him. We make it inside and to the stairs before he leans into me.

"You got him?" Jake asks.

"Yeah," I say. When we make it to the dorm, I lead Matt over to his bed. He sits gingerly.

"Thanks." He glances up at me.

I just smile in response, afraid he'll notice how out of breath I am from the exertion.

"Heather, sorry for snapping," he says, wincing.

"All's forgiven," she says.

We divvy up the food and eat in silence, Matt popping a few Advil with his dinner. Once I'm done eating, I clear Matt's paperwork from his bed. Matt stands up, slowly and painfully.

"Where do you think you're going?" I ask.

"With you," he answers, as if it's a no-brainer.

"Oh no you're not," I say firmly.

"The pharmacy will probably need my insurance card, and you don't know my birthday or anything," he says.

"Still, I'll figure something out. You need to stay."

Matt hobbles over to the door and cracks it open. "You coming?" he asks.

I reluctantly follow him out the door, Heather and Jake watching from the doorway. "I think I can figure it out without you," I say. He continues on. "Matt," I scold, crossing my arms.

"Kelsey, I would really like meds tonight," he says through gritted teeth, clearly in pain. "So you can drive, or I'll go myself. But one way or the other, I will be there." He glares at me.

"Fine. Let's go," I huff.

"I can come too," Jake pipes up from behind.

"We're good," Matt calls back, starting to walk again. I look back, and Jake shrugs.

Heather's brow furrows. *You got him?* she mouths. I nod.

Once outside, I instruct Matt to sit on the bench while I get my car.

"How far is it?" Matt asks, looking like he's contemplating walking with me.

"Farther than Heather's," I assure him, falling into a jog. "Sit tight. I'll be back."

When I pull up to the dorm, Matt is still sitting on the bench. I watch from the driver's seat as he gets up, grimacing. Poor guy.

"Thanks for driving," he says, sliding into the passenger side.

"No problem," I say.

"How are you doing?" he asks.

"Good. I wasn't the one in an accident." I give him a pointed look.

"I know, but you should have seen your face in the hospital. Pure white."

"It was not."

"It was."

"I was fine. I *am* fine." I'm hit with a jolt of realization. "Wait, is that why you told the nurse your pain level was a six? You didn't want to scare me?"

He winces. "Kind of. I thought if I answered honestly, you would have fainted."

"I wouldn't have."

"You looked like a ghost."

"I did not look that bad," I say defensively.

"Like Casper's twin," he retorts.

I think back to the clerk's worried look and the nurse's panic that I might be in shock. "Whatever, you could have answered honestly. You *should* have."

"And Kelsey faints. She awakens on a gurney next to a handsome young man…" he says theatrically.

"Stop it," I say, casting him a playful glare.

"Eyes on the road, please."

I face the road. "So?"

"So, what?"

"On a scale of one to ten, where was your pain?"

"Kelsey, don't worry about it."

"Just answer the question."

"Ten." He pauses. "And a half."

I tighten my grip on the steering wheel. "And now?"

"Honestly, the Advil is helping," he answers.

"That's not a number." I see the pharmacy up ahead and make the turn when he answers hesitantly.

"Nine."

"A nine!" I yell. "I cannot believe you. You are such an idiot! Trying to be tough just because I was in the room." I park the car and get out, slamming my door. His door opens, and he leans on the hood of my car, glowering at me.

"White, Kelsey. White! You looked horrid."

"Thanks," I snip and cross my arms.

"Look at me and tell me you were fine today. Truly fine."

I lock eyes with him but say nothing.

"I knew that hearing 'accident' and 'hospital' wasn't going to be easy for you. I didn't want you to relive any part of that day, but I could tell you still did."

"I was fine," I say, but Matt shakes his head. He pushes himself off the car and steps over to me.

"Are you sure you're okay?" he asks, taking my hand. I don't answer. I glance over at his right wrist in its bright orange cast.

"I don't like the color," I say instead, looking up at him.

"What would have been better?"

"Neon pink." I smile.

"Manly."

"Would have been better than orange," I say. We start toward the doors.

Of course, Matt does need to be there to provide his birthday, his insurance card, and his driver's license. He gives me a smug look as the pharmacist enters the information. I roll my eyes.

When we get back to his dorm, Heather is gone, and it's just Jake in the room. He helps me settle Matt into bed.

"Thanks for being there today," Matt says, his eyes closed.

"Wouldn't have been anywhere else." I smile and squeeze his hand once more. "Let me know if you need anything."

"Mm-hmm."

"Night, Jake." I swing the door open and take one step out.

"Kelsey," Jake says, and I peer back in. "I don't know how tough today was for you, but I agree with Matt—thanks for being there."

I smile. "I'm just glad both of you are safe," I say, stealing one last glance at Matt before heading back to my dorm.

Fifteen

I'm walking down a long, white hallway with wooden doors on either side. All are closed except for one. When I peek in, I swear I see Matt. I step inside. It's definitely Matt lying in the bed, but his injuries are not his. They're McKenzie's. When I inch closer, Matt's good eye opens.

I jump, waking myself up. I rest a hand over my heart, which is pounding out staccato beats. Catching my breath, I glance over at McKenna. She's still fast asleep. I lie there, staring at the ceiling for several minutes, too afraid to close my eyes again. When it becomes clear I won't fall asleep again, I drag myself out of bed and get ready for the day. I decide to check on Matt. I knock quietly on the door, but I hear nothing on the other side. Maybe it's still too early. I back away, about to leave, when the door swings open.

"Hey, Kelsey," Jake whispers, stepping aside to let me in.

"Hi. How is he?" I ask, entering the room. Matt is still in bed, snoring softly.

"Not bad. He's been out since last night."

"How are you?" I whisper.

"Good. A little sore, but I'll survive. Hey, would you mind staying to make sure he takes it easy today? I have a class."

"Are you sure?" I pause.

Jake nods as he grabs his backpack. When he straightens and looks at me, he raises an eyebrow. "Everything all right?" he asks.

"Yep. I'm good," I say, trying to sound chipper. Jake still looks skeptical but doesn't pry. He waves on his way out.

I sit on their disc chair and pull out my laptop, opening my English paper. The little sleep I got starts to catch up with me, and when my eyelids droop, I give up, setting my laptop on Matt's desk. With a yawn, I curl up in the chair and doze off.

The hallway is the same, but there is a door cracked open at the end of the hall. Another door gapes open right beside me. I turn to peer inside. Matt is lying in the bed, again bearing McKenzie's wounds. I step in to check on him, and the door closes behind me. The beeping on Matt's heart monitor starts to slow.

"This isn't right," I say, looking around the room. I brave another step toward Matt. "You're okay, you're okay," I tell him. Someone faintly calls my name, but no one else is in the room, and Matt is still unconscious on the bed. "Please wake up."

The room blurs. Suddenly, it's McKenzie lying in the bed. I rush to her side as the monitor stops, and I scream. My scream jolts me awake.

"Kelsey, are you all right?" Matt asks. My eyes shoot open, and he comes into focus. He is sitting straight up, his muscles tense.

"Oh my gosh. I-I am so sorry!" I stammer.

"It's fine." His shoulders relax a little. "Are you okay?"

"Yeah. I am so sorry for waking you."

"It's no big deal. What were you dreaming about?"

"Don't worry about it. Go back to sleep."

"Kelsey, tell me what happened," he says sternly.

"It was seriously nothing," I lie. I grab my laptop, closing it.

"What did it have to do with McKenzie?" he asks.

I freeze. "What?"

"You said 'McKenzie' before you screamed. What did it have to do with McKenzie?"

"…Nothing."

"Why won't you tell me?" he growls.

"Because it's really nothing!" I practically shout.

"If it's fine and it's nothing, then tell me!" He raises his voice to match mine.

We sit there, staring at each other. Finally, his face softens. "You can tell me," he encourages.

We won't get anywhere like this. I suck in a shaky breath. "You were…" I clear my throat. "You were in a hospital bed, but you had all of McKenzie's injuries. The heart monitor slowed." My voice breaks. "Then it wasn't you. It was McKenzie. The heart monitor stopped, and that's when I screamed." I stare at the floor.

"I am so sorry. That sounds terrifying," Matt says gently. I just shrug.

"I should go," I say, turning to pack up my backpack. "I have class."

"Please stay. Talk to me."

"No. I should go."

"Hey." I hear the bed creak and then his hand falls on my shoulder. I turn to face him.

"Go back to bed. It's not a big deal, really," I say as I step around him.

"Will you come by after class?" he asks.

"I don't know," I say weakly. I thought being here would be better. I could see him, and I would know he was okay. Instead, the nightmare has only escalated and I woke him for no reason.

"If you need to talk, I'm here," he says.

I turn back around to see him sitting at the edge of the bed. He looks exhausted. "Do you need anything before I go?"

He shakes his head. "Nah, I'm good for now."

"Don't be brave. Take pain meds, rest a lot, drink lots of fluids," I instruct.

"Thanks, Nurse Lanter," he teases.

"I'm serious."

I say a quick goodbye and head for class. Halfway down the hall, I am tempted to turn around and go back. Maybe he shouldn't be alone right now. After weighing my options, I choose class. Matt should be okay by himself for a little while. Right? I waver at the exit door, about to change my mind and turn around, when it swings open.

"Sorry," I say, moving to let the person in.

"Hey, everything cool?" Jake asks.

I breathe a sigh of relief. "Yeah, are you headed to your room?"

"Sure am. How's Matt?"

"Good, I think. I…accidentally woke him up," I confess.

"Oh. I'm sure he's all right. I'll stick around for a little bit."

"Okay." I peek up at the stairs.

He smiles and pats my shoulder. "He's good, Kelsey."

I nod and head out the door. During astronomy, I try to focus, taking meticulous notes like Matt did for me. Unfortunately, since I'm sleep-deprived and worrying about Matt, concentrating is no easy task. After class, I check my phone for the umpteenth time. No messages. I amble back to my dorm and try to take a nap, but I can't fall asleep. Lying in bed, I text Jake to see how he is.

He's out, he responds, with the sleepy face emoji next to it. I set down my phone and pull out my astronomy book. I am halfway through the chapter when my phone chimes. I nearly dive for it.

Hey, what are you doing? Jake texts.

Nothing, I reply.

Want to come over, make sure he continues to take it easy?

Sure. I pack up my bag and head over.

When I knock on the door, Matt answers.

"What are you doing up?" I ask disapprovingly.

"What are you doing *here*?" He turns to Jake before I answer. "Did you text her?"

"You didn't answer my question," I say, hand on my hip.

"Maybe," Jake answers.

"I don't need a babysitter," he says, turning back to me. "I don't need a babysitter," he repeats matter-of-factly.

"Yeah, ya do." Jake pats Matt's shoulders. "The meds make him a little loopy," Jake informs me as he walks out the door. "He can take another dose in an hour or so."

"I'm fine," Matt yells at Jake. He just keeps walking down the hall. Matt turns to me. "I'm fine. I'm sure you have other things to do."

"I really don't," I answer, stepping inside the room. "Let's get you back to bed."

He rolls his eyes. "You really don't need to be here," he says, sitting on the edge of his bed at a slug's pace. Jeez, I feel like I'm watching him in slow motion.

"Well, I *am* here. Do you need anything?" I ask.

"Not right now." He adjusts his pillows and then reclines. "Do you have homework, or do you want to watch a movie?"

"I could watch something," I say, sliding the desk chair over.

"What are you doing?" he asks. I glance at the chair, then at him, like this should be self-explanatory. He shakes his head. "Just come sit on the bed."

I leave the chair and join him on the bed. Slowly, I lean back against the headboard, trying not to jostle the mattress.

"What should we watch?" I ask as Netflix loads on his laptop.

"Good question. What looks good?" He starts to scroll through movies.

"Ooh, *Mulan*," I say excitedly. He looks at me, raising an eyebrow. I clear my throat. "Or something else."

"*Mulan* is fine." Matt smiles.

"Are you sure? We can pick something else…" I say, but he's already pressed play.

Mulan and the troops have just stumbled upon the village the Huns have decimated when Matt shifts his body and sucks in a sharp breath, clearly hurting. I carefully climb off the bed and grab the prescription pain meds from his desk.

"I don't want those," he says. "Advil is fine."

"No, tough guy. You need the good stuff," I say.

"That stuff puts me to sleep. Advil is good for now."

"Your body needs rest."

"I have been resting."

"I'm not arguing with you," I say, snatching a bottle of water and walking back to the bed.

"I'm not taking it," he says defiantly.

"Yes, you are."

"Kels, I've been in bed all—" I give him a pointed look. "*Most* of the day," he amends. "I'll take the good stuff before bed, I promise. I want to stay awake for the end of the movie."

"All right," I concede. "If Advil doesn't help, I'm making you take this one." I hold up the pill bottle for emphasis.

"Fair," he grumbles as I crawl back onto the bed. I slide back to my spot, and he grimaces.

"Sorry," I say, picking up the Advil bottle from the nightstand.

He pops three in his mouth and takes a sip of water. He hits play, and the movie resumes. I try to watch the movie, but out of the corner of my eye, I notice Matt shifting positions. After a few minutes, I'm more focused on him than the movie.

"Stop watching me," he whispers, glancing at me.

"Are you sure you're…" I trail off when he shoots me a glare. I turn back to the screen. The end credits are rolling by the time Jake walks in.

"Hey, guys," Heather says, following him. "How ya doing, Matt?" she asks, plopping down on Jake's bed.

"Is that pizza?" Matt asks Jake, eyeing the telltale box.

"Why, yes it is," Jake says cheerily. "Want a slice?"

"Yes. I'm starving," Matt answers. "And a soda while you're at it."

Jake grabs a soda from the fridge and tosses it to Matt. Something clicks in me, and I catch it before it reaches him. The guys look surprised and slightly in awe at the catch.

"Why? Why would you do that?" I snap. I have no idea why I'm mad. It's as if the action triggered a protective reaction in me. I didn't want the can to slip and hit him. Not that Matt wouldn't be able to catch it. He may have caught it just fine.

"What's the big deal?" Jake asks.

"What if he didn't catch it? He's already hurt."

"Kels, I'm fine. Worst case, it would fall on the bed," Matt says, reaching for the can of soda. I jerk it away. He stares at me, bemused. I know I'm overreacting, but I can't seem to pull myself together. I slam the can down on his nightstand and hop off the bed, this time not caring if I jostle him. I just have to get out of the room.

"Kelsey," Matt calls out. I don't stop. Maybe it's because I've been thinking of McKenzie all day, or because I'm tired. But I'm livid. I can't get the picture of a can hitting Matt square in the face out of my head, which is absurd. It didn't even happen.

"Wait!" I hear Matt yell. I turn to see him hobbling down the hall.

"Go back to bed!" I holler at him.

"No," he yells back, still inching toward me.

"You're being ridiculous," I say, lowering my voice a little.

"So are you."

I sigh and meet him halfway, crossing my arms.

"What was that?" he asks, stopping.

"I don't know," I murmur.

"I could have caught it, and even if I didn't, nothing would have happened." We're both silent. "Now, you want to tell me what this is all about?"

"I honestly don't know. In my head, all I pictured was the can hitting you and I flipped."

"Wow, you give me no credit. I am a pro catcher."

"I'm sure you are." I train my eyes on the floor, completely embarrassed.

"Is there anything else?" he asks. I look into his brown eyes, and I can tell he knows there is. This morning proved that. I didn't want to talk about it then, and I don't want to talk about it now.

"No," I say instead.

"Can we go back to the room then?" he asks. I hesitate. I had an audience for this little meltdown, and I'm not excited to walk in and face them. Matt takes a step back toward the room, and I reluctantly join him. Jake and Heather look up from their pizza.

"Everything okay?" Heather asks.

"Yeah. Sorry about that," I say, heading over to the pizza box and grabbing a plate. Matt walks up behind me, and I feel his hand on the small of my back.

"Can you grab me a slice of pepperoni and a slice of cheese?" His hand slides off to pull a bottle of water and another soda from the fridge.

"You already have one." I point to the can on the nightstand.

"This one's for you." He smiles at me.

"I thought you were going to say you didn't want the one she shook up," Jake jokes. Heather elbows him in the side.

We spend the rest of the night talking about classes and plans for the weekend through mouthfuls of pizza crust and mozzarella. When I see Matt yawn out of the corner of my eye, I take it as my cue to leave.

"Thanks for hanging out with me," Matt says as I pick up my backpack.

"You're welcome. I can come by tomorrow with notes for you."

"I'll probably be at class," he comments. Three pairs of eyes narrow on him. "Woah, okay. No I won't."

"I'll swing by tomorrow," I say.

"Wait for me!" Heather calls. She gives Jake a quick kiss, then turns to wave at Matt before following me out. She barely waits until we're outside the door before asking, "So, what's up with you and Matt?"

"I don't know… Nothing," I say.

"It doesn't look like *nothing*. It looks like two people who are totally into each other."

I keep my mouth clamped shut, heat rising to my cheeks.

"Well?"

"Well, what?" I look at her.

"Are you?" I know what she wants to hear. Suppressing a smirk, I don't give her a straight answer, making her sweat a little.

"Am I what?" I try to look as clueless as possible.

"Are you *into him*?" she asks impatiently.

I shrug, relishing the moment.

"Seriously?"

I can't hold it in anymore. A smile slips out.

"I knew it. You and Matt." She claps her hands together.

"We aren't anything yet," I try to explain before she gets too excited.

"You guys should be, though. You two are so cute together."

"We're just friends. We haven't even gone out yet." As soon as the words leave my mouth, her face lights up.

"We can fix that," she says, the wheels clearly turning.

"What are you thinking?"

"Double date!" she squeals.

"I don't know," I mumble. I am pretty sure Matt is into me, but he hasn't asked me out or anything. What if he doesn't want to? But Heather is already five steps ahead of me and spouting out plans. At this rate, she'll have every detail figured out before we get to our dorm building.

"…and don't worry, I'll tell Jake to go easy on you."

I stop, the last part catching my attention. "What?"

Heather turns around. "The intentions speech."

"Intentions speech?" I repeat, completely lost.

"Yeah. 'What are your intentions with my boy, you better treat him right, yada yada,'" she says in a tone mimicking Jake's.

I just stare at her, unblinking. She cannot be serious.

"Matt gave me the speech when Jake and I started going out. I survived. Plus, you know someone who can put in a good word for you." She winks at me.

"That makes me feel *so* much better." I start moving again.

When I get to my room, McKenna is in bed. I quietly brush my teeth and change into my pajamas, but my mind is on Matt. He is so sweet and has been a great friend these past few months. I want to date him, I decide, but I'm also worried that dating will change our friendship. What if we break up? I am not sure I can lose another friend.

Sixteen

I wake up the next morning still exhausted, so I grab coffee before class to help me pay attention. Matt doesn't make it to class so I take meticulous notes. I send him a quick text between classes to see how he's doing. When my phone chimes, I assume it's him.

Instead, *McKenzie's 19th Birthday EXTRAVAGANZA* is displayed across my screen.

I stop dead in my tracks, causing the guy behind me to slam into me. He mutters a couple profanities as he dodges me, glaring back over his shoulder. I can't tear my eyes from my screen.

We started planning McKenzie's birthday a few months before the accident. It all started when she found these gold candle holders that she thought would be perfect for centerpieces. After all, it was her golden birthday. She pulled out her phone and looked at her calendar, deciding on a pool party during spring break. She put it in her phone and insisted I add it to my calendar as well.

College will be crazy, so we should make plans now, she reasoned. I saved the reminder, just to humor her.

I hadn't completely forgotten about it, but I had been trying to chase it from my mind. Now, here was the reminder, like a stiff slap in the face. My screen blurs as tears fill my eyes. I blink hard, turning off my phone and scurrying to my next class.

After the lecture, I head to Matt's room to drop off my notes from yesterday and check on him. When I get to his room, the door is cracked. I knock, but no one answers, so I push it open a few inches and call out. No one is here. I step inside and look around.

"Hey," Matt says behind me.

"Matt!" I squeak, jumping out of my skin. "What are you doing up?"

"Just got up to get a snack." He smiles and holds out a bag of Cheetos, but his face falls when he catches my eye. "Woah, what's wrong?"

I hold out my phone, the notification still displayed on the screen. A tear snakes down my cheek.

"Oh." He steps closer to wrap me in a hug, his cast pressing against my back. I cry harder as he stands there, holding me.

"Want to talk about it?" he asks. I inhale sharply, and he continues, "It's okay if you don't, but I do think it would help."

"I was trying not to think about it." My voice is shaky. "I thought maybe if I wasn't mulling over it, then everything would be easier. It wouldn't—" The words catch in my throat. "It wouldn't hurt so much," I whisper. "I'm sorry."

"For what?"

"For this," I say, wiping my eyes.

"Kelsey, you have nothing to apologize for." He sits on his bed, scooting back to lean against the wall. He pats the covers and I sit beside him. "Talk to me. Please. When is her birthday?"

"March nineteenth. It's her golden birthday."

"What did you have planned?"

I gather myself before answering. "She was going to do a pool party at Justin's house. He was her boyfriend. She had golden candle holders and had found gold-colored streamers and tablecloths. She thought the candlelight would be pretty." I stare at my lap.

"Sounds awesome. Very golden," Matt comments.

"It would have been. She probably would have photographed everything too."

"You could still celebrate," Matt suggests.

"Why?"

"To remember her. It doesn't have to be big."

"I don't know…"

"It's just a thought. We did a cake for my brother. It was nice to celebrate with the family. It wasn't easy, but it was nice."

"I'll think about it," I say, letting the silence stretch between us.

The door swings open, and Heather struts in. "Friday! Get ready to wow Kelsey—" She pauses mid-sentence, her mouth dropping open to find that Matt isn't alone.

"Hi," I say awkwardly.

"I-I didn't know you were here," she tells me.

"Does he think it's a good idea?" Jake asks, walking in. His eyes bulge when they land on me. "Oh. Hey, Kelsey." He clears his throat and glances over at Heather.

"What am I missing?" Matt asks, eyes on Heather.

Heather bites her lip, probably contemplating how to answer without spoiling anything for me.

"Should I leave?" I ask. Heather nods.

"She doesn't have to leave," Matt protests as I climb off his bed.

"For two seconds," Heather says, pushing me out of the room.

"Really?" I hear Matt say as the door clicks shut.

I sit on the hallway floor with the sneaking suspicion that Heather is filling Matt in on our first date. I lean against the door, hoping to eavesdrop, but she must be keeping her voice down. It seems to take forever before the door opens again. I almost fall backward, and Heather looks down at me with a frown.

"I didn't hear anything," I blurt, standing. She eyes me suspiciously as I follow her in. I look over at Matt, who opens his mouth.

"Not a word," Heather orders. Matt mimes zipping his lips, locking them, and throwing away the key. When I sit next to him, he leans over and whispers, "I'll tell you later," with a wink.

Everyone starts working on homework. I wait for Heather to leave so I can hear the plans for Friday night, but it's like she has this sixth sense and refuses to leave us alone. I give up and tell the boys good night. Heather follows me out, and we walk together back to our dorm.

"So, Friday?" I prompt.

"No details. You just have to wait and see." A grin tugs at her lips.

When Friday comes, I still have no idea what we're doing. Matt doesn't give anything away in class, to my disappointment. Heather is waiting at my door when I arrive from class.

"Hey," I say, unlocking my door. "What's up?"

"We have to get ready." She plops down on my bed.

"Do I get to know what we're doing?" I ask, to which she shakes her head. I place my hands on my hips. "How will I know what to wear?"

"That's why I'm here. This way, I can give you input."

I huff. "I don't see why you can't just tell me."

"Sorry Charlie." She shrugs.

After finishing my shower, I stand in sweats and a tank, staring at my closet while Heather applies her makeup. She looks over, pointing with her eyeliner. "What about the jean skirt?"

I turn and make a face.

"You can't wear *that*," she says, gesturing to my current outfit before turning her attention back to her makeup. She finishes her eyes before coming over to study my wardrobe. Pulling out a deep purple blouse and setting it on my bed, she turns back to the closet and sighs.

"My wardrobe is not that bad," I say defensively.

"Is this everything?" she asks.

I walk over to my desk and roll out a plastic three-tiered drawer. "Will this help?"

"Perfect. Let's see what we've got." She starts pulling out pieces I haven't worn in months—mainly because I have been living in sweaters and yoga pants all semester. "Yes! This will look amazing." She turns, holding a gray maxi skirt. I immediately recognize it.

"Not that one," I state.

"What? Why?" She tilts her head, confused.

I don't want to tell her it wasn't mine. It's the same one McKenzie let me borrow two days before her accident. The one I was supposed to wear that night before having a last-minute change of mind.

"I think the jean skirt will be fine," I say instead, turning back to my closet.

"This one is so much better. It's so perfect for tonight; you have no idea."

I whip around to face her. "You're right. I have no idea. You won't tell me what we're doing. I just don't want to wear it."

Her nostrils flare as she inhales sharply. "Fine." She drops the skirt on my bed. "Just wear whatever. The boys should be here soon, so choose fast." She marches out of my room without looking back.

I glance over at my bed. The skirt is balled up next to the shirt. The colors do look nice together, and I'm sure it would look amazing on me. I walk over and change into my shirt. Heather comes back a few minutes later, popping open a can of soda.

"You don't have to wear it," she says, taking a sip.

"No, you're right. It looks good together."

"I'm sure the jean skirt would be fine too." She still has an edge to her voice.

"It's not mine," I say. She gives me a perplexed look. "The skirt. It's not mine. It's McKenzie's. Or…was."

"Oh. I didn't know." Her face softens.

"I know. I'm sorry for snapping."

"You really don't have to wear it."

"It's fine." A soft smile curves my lips as I brush the fabric. "She always said it looked better on me. That's why she let me borrow it."

I get changed, adding a little makeup on when McKenna walks in. "Wow! That skirt is beautiful."

"Thanks," I say.

"Big date?" she asks.

"Yes," Heather answers for me, smiling.

"With Photography Guy," McKenna says with confidence. So, this was an obvious connection. My blush is answer enough. "Good for you."

"McKenzie was right. That skirt looks fierce on you," Heather says.

Fifteen minutes later, we are both sitting on my bed, waiting for the guys to arrive. Heather glances at the door for the third time, then checks her phone. "Do you have any messages?" I pull my phone out of my clutch. I shake my head.

"They should be here by now," Heather says, brow furrowed as she checks her phone again. Is she worried?

"I'm sure they'll be here soon," I try to assure her.

"I hope so. Jake is always freakishly on time. This is not like him."

A knock comes at the door, and Heather jumps up to answer it. Jake is standing there, alone. He looks miffed.

"Hey, babe, what's the matter?" Heather asks.

"We're late," he answers, clearly perturbed.

"It's okay. Gave us some extra prep time," Heather consoles him. Jake still looks annoyed. She kisses him on the cheek and intertwines her fingers with his, and he relaxes a little.

"Who's 'we'?" I ask as Matt walks up behind them.

"Hi," he says, stepping around Jake and Heather. He's wearing a forest green button-down shirt and deep brown dress slacks. Jake gives him a look that signals he is the reason they're late.

"You look incredible," Matt says, beaming at me. My cheeks flush.

"Thanks. You clean up nicely."

"Can we go now?" Jake snarls, pulling Matt out into the hall. I'm about to follow when McKenna calls my name. I spin around, and she gives me a thumbs-up.

"He looks good," she whispers. "Have fun."

"Thanks." I give her a little wave before joining the others in the hall.

Jake and Heather are walking in front of us. "What happened?" I ask Matt, falling in step with him.

"I may have fallen asleep when I was supposed to be getting ready," Matt admits.

"Oh." I study his face and the dark bags under his eyes. He still looks tired.

"I couldn't really show up without him, so I waited," Jake chimes in.

"If tonight isn't good, we can always…" I fizzle out when Heather shoots me a look of death.

"And waste such a beautiful outfit?" Matt says. "Never." I give him a soft smile.

"So, do I get to know where we're going?" I ask as we reach the car. Heather shakes her head as she climbs in the driver's seat. Jake takes the passenger side, and Matt and I slide into the back.

The first stop sign we pull up to, I notice Matt tense, but he keeps his composure. At the second one, he leans away from the door. I graze my hand along his arm. "You're okay," I whisper. I start to pull my hand away when he catches it, lacing his fingers through mine. I squeeze his hand gently.

Heather pulls up to another stop sign, making a complete stop before inching forward. A car approaches on our right. Matt squeezes my hand and sucks in a breath. We are halfway through the intersection when the other car stops. Matt jumps, his whole body tensing. My hand feels like it's being crushed, but I try not to make a sound.

"Yo, Matt. They stopped. We're good, man," Jake says, craning his neck to look at him. He doesn't have a clear view of Matt, but I do. He's petrified. "Matt?"

"Yeah?" Matt says, nostrils flaring with every breath.

"Ease up on the death grip you have on Kelsey's hand. She doesn't need a cast too." Immediately, Matt releases my hand.

"I am so sorry," he says.

"It's okay," I say, taking his hand again. Matt takes focused breaths and tries to relax his shoulders.

"I'm sorry, Matt. I didn't think about it. I could have gone a different way," Heather says as we hop out of the car and walk up to the restaurant.

"It's fine, really. I didn't think I would react that way."

When we get inside, Heather tells the hostess how many are in our party, and we move to the side while we wait. I try to wiggle my fingers discreetly to get the blood flowing again.

"How's your hand?" Matt asks, watching me.

"It's all right," I say, flexing my fingers.

He takes my hand in both of his, resting it on his cast and rubbing my fingers with his good hand. I look up to see his shoulders are still rigid.

When the hostess calls Heather's name, Matt gestures for me to walk in front of him, then holds my chair out for me before taking his seat. The best thing about Italian restaurants is the warm baskets of bread the wait staff bring to the table. By the time our food arrives, I'm already full. Matt takes his medicine with dinner, but I can't tell if it's the good stuff or just Advil. He catches me watching and mouths that he's fine. I look at him skeptically.

"So, Kels, no rehearsal tonight?" Jake asks.

"We took the night off since the basketball team has an away game," I explain.

"Do you wish you could travel with the team?" Heather asks.

"Sometimes, but not this time. They went to Iowa, and it's freezing there."

We spend the remainder of dinner talking about travel—where we've been and where we wish to go. Once we clean our plates, Jake takes care of the check while Heather asks if we are ready for phase two.

"There's a phase two?" I ask, glancing worriedly at Matt. Is that such a great idea? Matt was already exhausted for dinner.

"Of course there's a phase two. Now, it isn't as exciting as I wanted it to be, but you didn't think we were just doing dinner, did you?" she asks, standing.

I shrug. "I had no idea what was going to happen tonight." We all rise from the table and head for the door. When we get to the car, I catch Matt's gaze before hopping in. "Are you good?" I ask. He nods.

Phase two is a movie. The boys buy popcorn while Heather and I find some seats. Unfortunately, the theater is packed. Heather spots the only row with available seats and rushes up the stairs to claim them.

"Are you having a good time?" Heather asks.

I sit on her left. This way, Jake can sit next to her, and Matt can sit next to me. "Maybe we should have waited," I say.

"Why? You and Matt are clearly into each other."

"I know, but I wish he could have been feeling better."

A couple squeezes past us to take the seats next to Heather when she splays her hand across the seat and informs them it's taken. The woman rolls her eyes, and they look around for another pair of seats together. As they squeeze by us again to claim two chairs closer to the screen, I spot Matt and Jake walk in and wave.

"He's fine," Heather whispers as the boys reach us. I give her a doubtful look. Once Jake passes me and sits next to Heather, Matt takes his seat next to me and yawns. As the lights dim, I notice his eyelids drooping. Yeah, a movie is not the best idea.

The four of us share a bag of popcorn, and I let Matt have the armrest for his cast. I kind of wish I was sitting on the other side, or the cast was gone, so I could hold his hand. I glance down at his palm twice; the third time, Matt wiggles his fingers. I peek up at him and he flashes me a charming smile. He moves his arm and holds my hand with his pinky, resting his cast on my leg. I am so thankful we are in a dark theater—my cheeks are on fire.

Matt makes it through the whole movie, surprisingly. When we exit the theater, I ask Heather if there is a phase three. I don't think Matt can do much more. She shakes her head. When we get back to the dorms, we thank Heather for a great evening.

"If Kelsey's okay with it, I think we should take a little walk." He looks at me.

"I'm okay with it," I say.

"You two have fun." Heather winks at me.

Jake waves at us before taking Heather's hand and walking with her toward the dorms.

I meet Matt at the rear of the car. He takes my hand in his good one, and we start walking.

"You really do look beautiful."

"Thank you." I blush.

"Sorry about tonight. Our first date was supposed to be better than this."

"You didn't have a good time?" I ask, frowning a little.

"No, I did. I just…it was supposed to be better. The night should not have started out with me arriving late and then almost breaking your hand. Sorry again."

"There's always next time," I say with an encouraging smile.

Matt gasps in horror. "You don't need to be in a cast too," he teases.

I let out a small chuckle. "No, the next date."

"The next one?" he asks, intrigued.

"I mean…" I clear my throat. "If you want."

"I'm just teasing, Kelsey." He smiles as my cheeks start burning. "I want to. I promise to be well rested and not on drugs."

"Speaking of drugs," I start.

"Just Advil," he finishes, squeezing my hand gently. He snorts. "I should have offered you some." He holds up my hand for emphasis.

"I'm okay," I say with a giggle.

We walk around for a while before he drops me off at my dorm. "I promise next time will be much better," he says as he backs away.

"I'm going to hold you to that," I say. He waves and then turns. I close the door, a huge smile stretching from cheek to cheek.

McKenna walks out of the bathroom. "I take it things went well."

"Yes, they did."

"I'm glad," she says, crawling into bed.

"Me too," I sigh, remembering the feeling of Matt's hand in mine.

Seventeen

Before I know it, Matt asks me out on a date, just the two of us. I'm gushing with excitement. He takes me to Lou Mings. It may be our standby, but this time, it feels different. He's wearing a nice button-up T-shirt and black slacks, and I curled my hair and chose a navy blue dress. As we wait for our food, he asks me about my major.

"I've thought a lot about becoming a dance teacher," I say.

"That sounds fun. I can see you as a dance teacher."

"Thanks. I love dance, and when someone gets it and their face lights up, I think that's the best part of it all. What about you?"

"I don't know," he says. "I've been enjoying photography a lot, but what am I going to do with that?"

"Lots of things. Wedding photographer, the picture guy for schools, landscape photographer, product photographer, photographer for a magazine…" I pause, trying to think of more.

"You've put thought into this." He smiles.

"My best friend was a photographer," I point out, then go silent.

"From what you've said, she sounds like she was extremely talented."

I nod. Thankfully, Matt changes the subject. We chat more about the future, the conversation feeling so smooth and natural. I know I'm falling for him, and I don't want to stop.

As spring break approaches, I'm sleeping less and less. McKenzie appears in every one of my dreams. Sometimes, they play like pleasant memories, but every now and then, they morph into nightmares—McKenzie becoming pale, cuts appearing on her face. On a few days, I show up to class exhausted. I even start to nod off during a lecture or two. Matt's concerned look with the little wrinkle in his forehead returns. He asks me what's going on, and I continue to say I don't want to talk.

The whole campus seems to be buzzing with spring break plans. One afternoon at a coffee meetup with Matt, Jake, and Heather, the latter two are discussing plans. Matt interjects occasionally, but I sit quietly, sipping my coffee.

"Kelsey, what's your opinion?" Heather asks, looking at me expectantly.

"Huh?"

"The volcano tube? Good idea, bad idea?"

"I-I don't know," I say.

"It's spring break. Where is the excitement?" she asks, energy infused in every word.

"It died," I say flatly, getting up. All eyes are trained on me as I turn away. "I think I'm going to take off."

"Oh. All right," Heather says, surprised.

I'm halfway to my car when I hear footsteps behind me.

"Kels," Matt calls. I swing around. "Do you want to talk about anything?"

"Not really. I'm just not in a spring break mood. I don't even want it to be spring break. This sucks!" My voice catches.

"I know." He pulls me into a hug, his cast pressing into my back. I wrap my arms around his waist, trying to hold in my tears. "You know I'm here if you need anything," he says tenderly.

"I know." I pull away. "Right now, I think I just need time."

"Go get some rest. I'll check on you later."

"I appreciate that, but could you wait for me to text you?"

His face falls a little. "Okay. You know where to find me."

I nod and start back to my room. Over the next several days, I withdraw from everybody. Heather texts me several times to see if I want to meet up for coffee or grab lunch, and each time I decline. My mom calls a few times to check on me. I tell her I'm fine. Delia sends a text, and I ignore it. Finally, the day arrives.

I'm thankful McKenna is out of town for spring break and I have the room to myself. I slept horribly last night and have been crying on and off all morning. My mom called early in the morning, and I kept the conversation brief. Matt has been keeping his distance, just as I requested. I only received two text messages from him over the past few days.

I am curled up on my bed, knees tucked against my chest, when I hear a knock on the door. I don't want to get up to answer it. My eyes are red, my face blotchy—I look like a mess. I don't move, hoping whoever it is will just go away. That hope is dashed when another knock comes.

"Kelsey it's me." Matt's voice is muffled through the door. I groan. He sucks at giving me space. I miss him though, and I know he's concerned about me. I get up and answer the door.

"Hey." He gives me a sympathetic look. "I won't stay long. I wasn't sure what you had in your room, and I didn't think you would feel like leaving. So I brought some stuff." He holds up a grocery bag.

"Thanks," I say, swinging the door open. "You want to come in?"

"I don't have to."

"I know. I want you to."

Matt steps into my room and I close the door, sitting back on my bed and pulling my knees to my chest. Matt sets the bag down on my nightstand and sits next to me. Neither of us say anything. I sniffle, a few stubborn tears escaping. I turn to face the wall and rest my cheek on my knee, the bed creaking as Matt moves. He is still quiet, but his hand takes mine. I lace my fingers through his, and the tears fall harder. Eventually, snot starts dripping from my nose and I need to run to the bathroom for some tissue. I bring extra back to the bed. Matt waits through it all, his expression soft, until I'm ready to talk.

"What did you do today?" I ask.

"Ran a couple errands and convinced Heather not to come over."

"Heather wanted to come over?"

"She hasn't seen you lately and wasn't going to let you waste the whole week doing nothing," he explains.

"Oh." I rub the remaining moisture from my face.

"Don't worry. I told her I would talk to you and—oh, lookie here—we talked."

"If I don't do something with her this week, I'll make it up to her."

"Don't worry about it. She'll survive." He pauses. "So, how are you?"

"I don't know."

My phone rings before I can say more. Without thinking, I pick it up. "Hello?"

"Hey, sweetie," Delia says. "How are you doing?" Her voice sounds calm, even a tad cheery. I wonder if she is forcing it for my sake.

Too bad I can't muster up a happy tone for her. "I'm doing okay," I murmur, my voice cracking.

"What have you been up to? After all, it is spring break."

"Not much." I sniffle.

"I know this week is tough, today especially." Delia's voice catches. "I don't want you to sit around all weekend. She wouldn't have wanted you to, either."

"She doesn't get a say. She's not here," I snap.

"No, she's not." Delia's voice trembles. "Still, she wouldn't want you to sit in your room. She would tell you, 'You're going to miss all the little things.'" Delia starts to cry, and a tear rolls down my cheek too.

I add, "She would convince me that even if nothing exciting happened, *something* would happen, even if it was a tiny something."

"Exactly."

I sigh. "What made it fun, though, was that we were together."

"You're telling me there is no one up there to hang out with?"

"There is." I glance at Matt.

"So, get out. Go get a coffee, take a walk. You might miss something—even a tiny something—if you sit in your room." She adds, "John and I are going out tonight to celebrate her birthday."

"Really?" I ask, surprised.

"Yes. She was our baby and even though she isn't with us, we want to celebrate her."

"Someone mentioned celebrating her birthday to me too." Matt looks at me questioningly.

"It might help you. If you don't want to do it today, that's okay. But maybe sometime this week?"

"I'll think about it."

There's commotion on the other line, like the phone is being shuffled around. "Hi, Kelsey," I hear John say.

"Hi," I say, noticing a slight echo, like she put me on speakerphone.

"We miss you, kiddo."

"I miss you guys too."

"Call us any time," he says.

"Yes, any time," Delia agrees, closer to the phone.

"I know. I love you guys."

"We love you too. Remember to get out this week. Enjoy the little things."

"Okay," I say, my voice breaking again.

"Who was that?" Matt asks once I say goodbye and hang up.

"Delia. McKenzie's mom."

"You sound really close to her."

I nod. "She's like a second mom to me."

"You mentioned celebrating?" He raises an eyebrow.

"Yeah. They're going out tonight to celebrate her birthday, just like you suggested."

He pauses, absently drawing circles on the comforter with his finger. "Do you want to do something?"

"I don't know. It's really hard."

"I get that. But it might be good."

I ponder what Delia said about not sitting in my room all week. What would McKenzie have done if she were here? Well, it definitely wouldn't have been cramming herself in this stuffy room.

"Maybe going out wouldn't be so bad," I say.

"You don't have to if you don't want to," he says, squeezing my hand.

"But Delia's right. If McKenzie were here, we wouldn't be huddled on the bed for days on end. She would be too afraid we would miss something."

"What do you have in mind? And do you want company?"

"Not sure about the 'what' yet, but company would be nice." I smile at him, hopping off the bed to grab some clothes. "Give me a minute."

He nods. I step in the bathroom and shower, thinking of all the small things I would have missed if McKenzie and I had sat in the house instead of going out. Like the time Corey was at Starbucks with his new girlfriend a few weeks after we broke up, and McKenzie stuck her foot out, making him spill his coffee all over himself. I would have missed late-night drives around town, just getting things off our chests and listening to music. Some of the deepest conversations happened during those drives. I would have missed the smile on Justin's face that night at Sarah's party, and the smiles every day after. I would have missed McKenzie's signature giggle when he would surprise her with a cookie or coffee—all the little things that let me know she was falling for him, and him for her. My life would have been so boring without those moments.

I dry myself off, putting sweats back on and throwing my hair up in a messy bun. I cried in the shower, so my eyes are still red and puffy.

"Ready to get out of here?" I say, swinging my purse strap over my shoulder and checking to make sure I have my wallet. I grab my keys and head for the door, the bed creaking as Matt gets up. I pause at the door. Deep breath. *I can do this.*

I open the door and walk out. After I lock it behind us, he takes my hand, and we start for the exit.

"So, what was the original plan for today?" he asks.

"Coffee and pastries at Starbucks, mani-pedis, and shopping at the mall. Then we would've went to Justin's to set up for the party." I train my eyes on the floor, and Matt squeezes my hand.

"Do you want to do any of that?"

"Coffee sounds good."

"Coffee it is."

I order a caramel macchiato—McKenzie's favorite. I try to order without bursting into tears, and the barista looks at me as if one wrong word will set me off. Matt orders his coffee and pays.

"So, what about this drink made it McKenzie's favorite?"

"It is delicious hot or iced, it's simple, and it's always on the menu. So no matter where she went, they wouldn't screw it up."

"And yours is a vanilla latte?" he asks.

"Yeah. What about you?"

"I go for straight coffee. Every once in a while, I do one of those frozen drinks. What are they called?"

"Frappuccinos? Those are good too."

Once we finish our coffee, I have no idea what to do next. I don't realize I'm biting my bottom lip until Matt points it out.

"What are you thinking about?"

"I don't know where to go from here," I say.

"Well, you mentioned mani-pedis or the mall. Do you want to do one of those?" Since I can't see Matt getting a mani-pedi, I opt for the mall. As we stroll down the concourse, Matt fusses with his cast.

"What is going on?" I ask, giggling.

"It itches," he complains. It had been bugging him for a few weeks now. I had seen him shove a chopstick, a spoon, and in class, an unsharpened pencil to scratch it.

"When do you get it off?"

"Next week. It's so far away," he whines. He rubs his cast like his hand will somehow pass through it and scratch his arm.

"I thought you weren't a complainer when you're sick," I comment.

"I'm not sick."

"So, only when you're injured do you turn into a baby?"

"Hey, I haven't complained much," he says with a huff, and it's true.

I drag my step until my shoe squeaks on the polished floor. "So, what does Heather have planned this week?"

"I think she has an activity planned for every day. Why do you ask?" He glances my way as I veer toward a store full of scented lotions and body scrubs.

"She wanted me to hang out, right?" I pick up a bottle of lotion, popping the cap to sniff.

"Yeah, but there's no pressure."

I set down the bottle and meander a few shelves over. Without paying attention, I pick up a bottle of one of their classic scents and take a whiff. It smells just like McKenzie. She loved this scent. She must have gotten a bottle every birthday and holiday for a solid two years. The scent brings up too many memories, and I shove the bottle back on the shelf, knocking a few bottles over. Feeling like the wind has been knocked out of me, I bolt out of the store, leaving Matt behind. The mall was a bad idea—this whole thing was a bad idea.

"Woah, Kelsey," Matt says, catching up to me. He grabs my arm, stepping in front of me as tears threaten to spill down my cheeks. He starts to pull me into a hug, but I push him away.

"Not here," I say, stepping around him and scurrying toward the doors to the parking lot. When I reach his truck, I cover my face with my hands and let my emotions run raw. He wraps me in a tight embrace. Once the wave of tears recedes, we climb into his truck.

"Do you want to go back to the dorm?" he asks. I just nod.

We are halfway back when I spot a grocery store. "Hey, can we make one more stop?"

He glances over at me. "You sure?"

"Yeah, I'd like to stop somewhere for cake."

Matt pulls into the parking lot. Once inside, I head straight for the bakery section. I scan the selection of individual cake slices, spotting one with little yellow flowers in the corner. I pick it up, taking it to the counter and asking if they can write "Happy 19th M" on it. My throat feels tight, but I keep my composure. It's a tight fit, but the lady does it.

Once we're back on campus, Matt walks me to my dorm.

"Do you want some cake?" I ask, holding out the slice.

He hesitates at the doorway. "Do you want me to stay?"

"Yes," I say assuredly. He steps in and closes the door. I grab two forks and sit on my bed, snapping a picture of the cake and sending it to Delia before biting into it.

I swallow the mouthful of buttery frosting. "I think she would have liked you."

"You think so?"

"Not at first. She would have made you work for me…but eventually."

"Sounds like I would've liked her too, then." Matt smiles and takes a forkful of cake. "What's one of your favorite stories about her?"

I start giggling before I even start the story, recalling the moment. "Okay, so when Shelby was four, we all went to the zoo. Of course, McKenzie had her camera with her. She was taking pictures of the Fennec foxes, the small ones with the big ears. Shelby told McKenzie that she wished she could take one home.

"I should've known they were up to no good when they started whispering to each other, but then Shelby said, 'We could sneak in?' I started paying closer attention after that and I remember McKenzie saying, 'We should probably come when it's dark. We'll dress in black.' They were planning a full fox heist!

"It took days after the zoo trip before Shelby moved on. McKenzie gave Shelby a picture of the foxes to hang on her wall. It's still there." I chuckle.

"Did the fox heist ever take place?" Matt asks.

"Unfortunately—or maybe fortunately?—no. It was hysterical listening to them plan, though." I giggle at the memory. "Shelby even taught McKenzie how they were going to tiptoe in." I get up and demonstrate how to properly sneak—up on my tiptoes, elbows pulled close to my side, hand sticking out.

Matt laughs until his shoulders shake. "She sounds like a great friend."

"She was the best." I sit back down, and a yawn escapes before I can stifle it.

He smiles softly. "I'll take that as my cue to leave."

"You don't have to," I say. "Want to watch something?"

He pauses for a moment before lifting his shoulders. "Sure."

I open my laptop and pull up Netflix. We pick a show, and I hit play. Matt scoots closer to me, draping his arm around my neck. I lean into him, resting my head on his shoulder. Before I know it, I'm asleep.

I'm in a hospital room again, and Matt is lying in the bed, tubes snaking from his body. I edge over to the bed and take his hand, squeezing gently. "You can't leave me," I say. The heart monitor pulses with an irregular heartbeat. "Please, wake up."

The heart monitor slows, beeps a few times, and then falls to a steady hum.

I jerk awake, gasping for air.

"Woah, you're okay. You're safe," Matt whispers, holding me tight.

I gulp for air, and it takes me a moment to get a full breath. When I look over at Matt, the little crease in his forehead is deep.

"I'm all right," I say through heaving breaths.

"You scared the crap out of me. Was that a nightmare?"

I nod.

"I thought the one you had in my room was bad. Does this happen a lot?"

"It's been happening more often," I admit.

"This is why you've been so tired." He brushes a sweaty lock from my forehead. "Have you considered what I said about talking to someone?"

I shrug. "I don't know."

"I really think you should. This is bad."

I feel a grin tease my lips.

"Why are you smiling?"

"You're worried."

"Of course I'm worried. As your—" Matt clamps his mouth shut.

"As my…?" I wait, but he doesn't continue. "What were you going to say?"

Matt inhales. "As your…boyfriend, I will always worry about you." He shakes his head, backtracking. "Okay, I don't even know where that came from. We haven't talked about it. I mean, we've only been on two dates, and one was a group date, so I don't even know if that counts…"

My grin stretches wider as Matt rambles on.

"What?"

"Your girlfriend thinks you're quite adorable."

His eyes widen, his mouth slightly agape. "My girlfriend?"

"Yeah."

Matt's jubilant smile could light up a city. "Well, your *boyfriend* does think it would be a good idea to talk to a counselor, or someone."

"Well, your girlfriend takes that under advisement. She is so sorry for scaring you."

Matt wraps me in a sweet embrace, and I slip my hands around his waist. He murmurs into my hair, "I'm serious about counseling."

"I know. I'll think about it."

Just then, my phone chimes with a couple of text messages from Delia. She found the gold cupcake wrappers McKenzie had purchased and made cupcakes. After going out for a nice dinner, they enjoyed the dessert and coffee by the fire pit. The texts bring up bittersweet feelings. McKenzie isn't here, but I'm happy to know she will always be remembered.

Even though months have passed, time has not healed this wound completely. I'm not sure it ever will, if this ache will ever go away.

"Does it get better?" I ask Matt.

His warm brown eyes fill with tenderness. "It gets easier."

Eighteen

Pool day?

I wake to Heather's text. She's messaged me several times since yesterday, and I feel bad for not responding. I could spend another day in my room, or… I glance at the door. Who knows what little things could happen? I text Heather and ask how to get to the pool. She sends me a smiley face emoji and the directions.

"Hey! Long time no see!" Heather waves her arms wildly when she sees me, Jake standing next to her.

"I know. Sorry," I say when I reach them.

"You've been *incommunicado* for a while now," she points out, sounding a little bummed.

"I know." I scratch my arm, feeling a little embarrassed. "Yesterday was McKenzie's birthday, and I was having a rough time."

"I didn't know that. I am so sorry." She gives me a hug. "Do you need anything? Do you want to talk?"

"I think I want to swim."

"Let's do it." She smiles, skipping toward the entrance.

After finding a spot on the grass and laying our towels out, the three of us look out at the crisp blue water glimmering under the Arizona sun.

"You actually have to get in the water to enjoy it," Matt's voice calls from behind us.

"What's up?" Jake greets him with a fist bump as he joins our group.

"Not much. Came to work on my tan," Matt replies. He slides what appears to be a camera bag off his shoulder.

"That is going to be one weird tan," Heather says, pointing to his bright orange cast.

"Yeah. Why *are* you here?" I ask. He can't swim in that cast, and the thought of a tan demarking the contraption isn't exactly appealing.

Matt fakes an incredulous look. "Ouch. I'm hurt."

"Sorry, I didn't mean it like that. You just can't get in the water."

"True, but I can hang out. Everyone else is here. You're here." He catches one of my stray locks and smooths it back into place. I smile.

Heather fake gags at the show of affection. "Whatever. I'm going in," she announces, strutting to the edge of the pool. She stands there a moment before jumping in, a splash rising in her wake.

Jake inches toward the pool, peering over the edge. "How's the water?" he asks when she emerges.

I shake my head when we hear a splash.

"Hey!" Jake's legs are now dripping while Heather backstrokes away from the pool ledge, grinning. "You're gonna get it!" he threatens, jumping in.

Their splashes and laughing fade into the background as I sit by Matt.

He turns to me. "You getting in?"

"In a bit. For now, I can keep you company."

"You don't have to."

"Fine. I can work on my tan." I lie on the scratchy cotton of the old beach towel and close my eyes, the sun warming my skin.

"Did you sleep okay last night?" he asks. I shrug one shoulder. Last night wasn't horrible, but I did have some vivid dreams. McKenzie was there, dressed in a gold dress. Sometimes she looked healthy, full of color. Other times she had a scar on her forehead and looked ghostly pale. From the corner of my eye, I catch Matt scrutinizing my face.

"If you want, I can introduce you to a woman at church. She leads the grief group and is a licensed therapist."

I mull over the idea, imagining spilling my guts to a therapist. And stepping into a church again. Am I ready for that?

When I don't respond right away, Matt looks nervous, like he crossed a line. "Maybe it's too—"

"No, I'll meet with her," I say before I can take it back.

Matt tears his eyes from me, facing the pool. "The water looks so nice." He sounds jealous.

"Yeah. You could stick your feet in," I suggest.

"Maybe. It's just not the same." I close my eyes, the sunlight turning the backs of my eyelids red, when I hear Matt ask, "So, when are you getting in?"

I open my eyes. "In a little bit."

"Are you scared?"

"No. If you're sick of me, though, I can leave."

"Well…" he teases.

I scoff. "Fine!" I jump up and march to the edge of the pool.

"Yay!" Heather cheers from the water.

I am trying to decide if I want to ease in or just jump when I feel two warm hands on my back. "Let me help you," Matt says, pushing me in. I fall through the air, break the surface, and hold my breath as cool water engulfs my body.

"You jerk!" I yell once I surface, sputtering water. Matt is laughing, which makes me want to splash him. "You will pay." I throw him a menacing look, to which he laughs harder.

"That was great," Heather giggles as she swims over to me. I turn and splash her.

"Hey! I didn't push you," she says defensively, splashing me back.

"You laughed."

Matt sits on the ledge and sticks his feet in the water. "So, how is it?" I ask, hanging on the ledge beside him.

"Feels good," he says. He looks so bummed he cannot slide all the way in.

"One more week." I give him a pat on the knee.

"That's so long." He hangs his head.

After we swim around for a few minutes, Matt eventually stands and walks over to our towels. He kneels and grabs his camera. I swim over to the ledge, about to offer that I can come back out, when I see him taking a few pictures of our towels, every once in a while folding a corner or moving our bags. Eventually, he makes his way back to the ledge, snapping some pictures of the rippling water and the crowded pool. He fiddles with the zoom, lens trained on Jake and Heather. His eyes are bright with excitement. A smile spreads across my face. It brings me so much joy to see him happy.

Once we have had our fill of splashing around and accidentally swallowing chlorine water, we grab some food and head back to the boys' dorm. I had taken a couple of pictures at the pool, so I send them to Delia. She is happy to see I'm out, but especially makes note of the fact I am with a boy.

Is this the boy you mentioned over Christmas?

Yes, I type back. She sends a little drooling emoji.

I approve, looks-wise. I'm gonna have to meet him before I make any official decision.

One day.

Jake hooks up his laptop to his large computer monitor and we use the screen as a makeshift television to watch Netflix. Between the delicious food and the sun, I'm beat. Once Matt is finished with his food, I snuggle into his side. He loops his arm around me, and I slowly drift off.

From the sidewalk, I see McKenzie's smashed car. The crescent-shaped door lies in the middle of the intersection, but the color reminds me more of Jake's car. I check my surroundings and begin to walk over to the door, inspecting it. Movement catches my eye, and I glance over. McKenzie's leaning on the scrunched hood of her car. Her complexion is perfect.

"You know what sucks?" she asks me.

I shake my head.

"He gets to leave." She nods to the other side of the intersection. When I turn, I see Matt standing on the corner. He lifts his hand, sporting a tie-dye pink and orange cast, and waves. I turn back to McKenzie, who suddenly loses all her color.

I startle awake. Matt immediately tightens his grip on me.

"You okay there?" Jake chuckles.

"Was it one of those dreams where you feel like you're falling? I hate those," Heather says.

"It wasn't that," I say. "Those are the worst though."

When I peek up at Matt, his eyes are trained on me. The little worry crease is etched deep in his forehead.

I'm good, I mouth before leaning back into him. I turn my attention to the screen and watch the rest of the show.

When the credits begin to roll, I stand and say my goodbyes. Matt offers to walk me back to my dorm.

Once in the hall, Matt takes my hand. "So, how are you feeling?"

"I'm doing okay," I say. "I had fun today."

"Glad to hear it." He takes a breath. "What was your dream about?"

We walk silently for a moment.

"We were at the intersection. McKenzie's car was wrapped around the light pole. There was a door in the middle of the intersection, but it was the wrong color." I describe my dream and then fall silent.

"That's some pretty vivid detail."

"Well, the scene is a little hard to forget."

Matt stops us. "Wait, you were there?"

"I was on my way to the party when I spotted the accident." A lump forms in my throat, making it hard to swallow.

"Oh my gosh. Kelsey, why didn't you tell me?"

I clear my throat. "Why would I?"

He gives my hand a squeeze. "It just seems like a big part of your story. That had to have had an impact."

I flinch at the word *impact*.

"Sorry," Matt whispers. He studies me a moment, digesting this new piece of information. A hint of the crease appears on his forehead.

"You don't have to worry. I'm okay."

"All right. Just know I'm always here for you," he says, beginning our walk back to my dorm.

The next day, Heather calls and asks if I have plans that evening.

"No, not that I can think of."

"Cool. You should come with us," she says.

I raise an eyebrow. "Where?"

I hear the smile in her voice. "That's a surprise. Be out front by eleven."

"*At night*?" I ask. What on earth could be happening that late? "Can I get a hint what we'll be doing?"

"Nope! See you tonight," she sing-songs into the phone and then hangs up.

At a quarter till eleven, I'm standing outside, waiting. Jake walks into the parking lot carrying a handful of blankets.

"Good evening," Heather greets me from behind. "You ready?"

I turn, still trying to figure this whole thing out. "I don't know," I say honestly.

She heads to the car, walking backward to talk to me, and I follow. "It's going to be awesome, trust me." She backs right into Matt. He turns, about to say something when he spots me.

"Oh, hi." He smiles. "Glad to see you."

"You too." Heat rushes to my cheeks, which seems silly since we saw each other just yesterday.

"Car's packed," Jake announces as he closes the trunk. "We ready?"

We all load into the car, and to my surprise, Jake starts driving out of town. When we park, we're at the foot of a wooded trail. Several other cars are parked nearby, and I notice a few people grabbing blankets and flashlights out of their trunks.

"What are we doing here?" I ask as we reach the trailhead.

"You'll see." Matt offers me his hand. I take it and let him lead me into the maze of conifers and pine trees. We reach a clearing, where several people have laid out blankets or sit in fold-out chairs. I help spread out the blankets, and the three of them lie back.

"What are we doing?" I ask again, hoping someone might answer.

"Just lay down. You'll see," Heather whispers back.

I sit on the blanket and look up at the stars. It's pitch black out here and the sky is clear, creating a natural window to every galaxy of the star-dappled sky. I watch for a minute. I open my mouth, about to start demanding answers, when I catch it—a bright streak across the sky. I keep watching and see another one.

"Wow," I breathe.

"I know," Matt whispers beside me.

A blanket of cool air descends on the woods, and I didn't come prepared. I shiver.

"You cold?" Matt asks.

"A little."

"Move closer," he whispers.

I scoot toward him, and he drapes his arm around me. I curl into his side, laying my head on his shoulder. It's late, but I don't know how late. My eyelids are growing heavier by the minute.

"You're missing it," Matt whispers in my ear. I open my eyes and try to watch. More meteors are streaking across the sky now than when we first arrived, but it's not enough to keep me awake. The next thing I know, Matt is gently shaking me. I sit up and rub my eyes, surprised by the dreamless sleep. It looks like several people have left, though some are still watching. Most of our stuff is all packed up. Matt extends his hand, and I let him pull me up so Heather can grab the blanket.

We trek back to the car. When we get there, I lean against the hood, yawning. We climb in, and Matt pats his leg. Taking him up on his silent offer, I lie down. I'm out before Heather puts the car in reverse.

"Kelsey," Matt whispers. When I wake again, I feel groggy.

"Are we back?" I rub my eyes.

"Yes. Let's get you to bed." Crawling out of the car and stretching, we walk hand in hand back to my dorm.

At my door, I turn to look into his eyes. "Thanks for walking me back."

"Of course. I hope you enjoyed tonight."

"I did." I smile at him.

"Good. You know, I like it when you smile," he says, which makes me smile bigger.

He gives me a hug and then pulls away slightly, his good arm still wrapped around my waist. Gazing into my eyes, he leans in and kisses me. A shot of adrenaline spikes through my limbs, tickles my nerve endings. My stomach flutters and flips. Did he really just…?

He pulls away, and the smile on his face rivals the brightness of the meteors. "Night, Kelsey," he says, releasing me. I don't say anything. I don't even think I'm breathing. He is halfway down the hall when I finally call out a goodnight.

Nineteen

On Sunday morning, I glance at the clock, debating. If I leave in the next five minutes, I'll make it to church.

Before I can change my mind again, I spring out of bed.

After throwing my entire closet on the floor in a desperate attempt to find something to wear, eventually settling on a dress-casual outfit, I hop in the car and drive to church. Stepping into the sanctuary, I look around, spotting Matt talking to a young couple. As I approach, Matt notices me and his eyes widen to saucers. He finishes his conversation and then excuses himself.

"What are you doing here?" Matt asks as we search for a seat.

"I honestly don't know. It was kind of a last-minute decision."

We spot Jake and squeeze through the row to take a seat next to him. Heather finds us as the lights are dimming. She leans down to give me a quick hug before moving to her seat. The music starts, and the worship leaders ask everyone to stand.

Can I really go through with this? My heartbeat quickens, while my hands glisten with sweat. This may have all been a big mistake—

again. Matt glances at me. I'm about to stand with everyone when Matt sits down again.

"Hey, I know last time was rough, and if you don't think you can do this…" I start to explain when he holds up his hand. "It's fine. You don't have to stand or sing, and if you need to walk out for a moment, feel free. Just don't leave the premises, okay?" I nod. He studies me for a moment before standing back up. I follow suit.

The first two songs don't rattle me. I even sing along with the second. When the notes of the third song play, I freeze. I don't know what it is about "King of My Heart," but it's the same one they played last time I was here—the song that caused the meltdown. Matt glances over at me, and Heather peers around the boys to check on me. I inhale through my nose but stay where I am, listening to the song without singing along.

Tears gather in my eyes. I glance down, wishing Matt didn't have a cast on this hand. I wrap my pinky around his, my whole body still as the worship band repeats the chorus. Something about this song stirs my heart. Then, a thought enters my mind, unrelenting. Maybe I'm shutting God out when He wants to pull me close. Maybe He's been holding me this whole time, like the song says, and I've been too angry to feel His presence.

I make it through the entire service, not once having to leave. The church has a charismatic pastor, and the message is encouraging. I can see myself attending regularly.

"You made it through the whole thing," Jake comments as we walk out. Heather smacks his arm. "What did you think?" he asks, giving Heather a glare.

"I thought it was really good."

"Cool. So, should we expect you next week?" he asks.

I tilt my head, lifting one shoulder in a shrug. "Maybe." I see Matt grin before glancing around the sanctuary.

"Oh, hey." He tugs my arm. I follow him to a woman in a floral sundress and denim jacket. She has pin-straight black hair. "Mrs. Carter," Matt calls.

She smiles when she sees him. "Why, hello!" she says as we approach. "How are you this fine morning?"

"I'm good," Matt responds. "I wanted to introduce you to my girlfriend, Kelsey." His smile widens as he says *girlfriend*.

"Nice to meet you." She extends her hand. "I'm Melissa Carter."

"Kelsey." I shake her hand.

"Are you still leading the grief group?" Matt asks.

"Yes. We're meeting Wednesday nights." Mrs. Carter glances between the two of us, clearly looking for some explanation.

"I lost my best friend a few months ago," I explain. "Matt thought it would be a good idea for us to meet."

"Aw, I'm sorry to hear about your loss. Well, we would love to have you. There is something about sharing your story that is very healing." She must sense my apprehension because she quickly adds, "If you would like, we can meet one-on-one first. I can tell you about the group and get to know you a little better."

"I'd like that."

Mrs. Carter digs in her purse and pulls out a card. "Call me anytime, and we'll arrange something."

"Thanks." I look over the information before slipping the card in my purse.

After saying our goodbyes, we head for the courtyard where Jake and Heather are standing around chatting and make plans for lunch.

The rest of our Sunday is relaxing, but in the back of my mind, I remember that classes start up again tomorrow. I'm ready to jump back in, but also nervous. In just a few months, my freshman year of college will be over.

On Monday, my grumbling stomach leads me to the dining hall to grab lunch before class. When I walk in, I spot Jake in line. There are two people behind him. I think about saying hi, but I stay quiet until Jake turns and notices me. He politely lets the couple go ahead of him.

"How goes it?" he asks.

"Pretty good. You?"

"Fueling up before my next class."

The guy at the counter takes our orders, and we sit down with our food. Funny. I think this is the first time we've been alone together since the night he scolded me after my outburst. It's quiet for a bit, just us eating our food.

"So, you and Matt," Jake says, breaking the silence.

"Yep." I smile, not thinking much of it. Then, Heather's comment about "the talk" crawls to the forefront of my thoughts.

"You do know Matt's my boy, right?" He gives me a hard stare.

"Yes." I smirk.

"This is not a funny moment. This is serious." His expression remains stern, and it takes everything in me to keep a straight face. I'm not doing a very good job. "I know he likes you and I'm glad he's found someone, but if you're going to be in his life, you'd better treat him right."

I nod. "I get it. 'Don't be a jerk, don't break his heart. If you break him, I break you,'" I say in a threatening manner.

"Woah. I'm not sure about the last part, but yeah."

"I had a best friend. When she started seeing someone—a mutual friend—I gave him the speech."

"You're good at it. But you sound a little scary when you deliver the last line, like you could do some real damage." Jake intertwines his hands behind his head, nodding in approval.

"Why, thank you. I meant it. I'm sure you would, too, if something happened to Matt."

"Yep, you pretty much summed it up. You hurt him, I hurt you." He pauses. "Didn't sound as menacing, did it?"

I shrug. "Eh, you can practice."

He gives me a look. "Do you think I need to?"

I smile and shake my head. "I plan on being around for a while."

"Good."

After the speech, we continue chatting between bites. My food is almost gone when two hands cover my eyes, causing me to jump.

"Guess who?" a voice says from behind me.

"Matthew Oliver Barker," I state.

"Dude, uncool," Matt scolds Jake. "You don't share middle names."

I grin. "Hey, your cast is off," I note.

"Why yes, Kelsey—I need your middle name—Lanter. It is." He sits beside me, wrapping his now free arm around my shoulders.

"How does it feel?"

"Weird." He wiggles his fingers. "What are you two up to?"

Jake and I share a look. "I...have to get going," he says quickly. "Kelsey, it was fun." He picks up his tray and heads for the door, waving as he leaves.

Matt snorts. "Well, you're still here, so I'm assuming he must approve."

I look at him incredulously. "You knew about the speech?"

"I knew it was coming. I took a guess since you guys were here alone."

I shake my head at their antics, getting up to take my tray to the trash. We walk out together and then part ways, me heading for my car. Halfway across the parking lot, I stop.

"Faith!" I yell out. He turns. "My middle name."

"Kelsey Faith Lanter," he says my full name and smiles. "Beautiful."

After rehearsal on Tuesday, Matt meets me for a late dinner.

"You look happy," he comments as we finish eating.

"Rehearsal was great. I had fun tonight."

He tilts his head, half smiling. "You know, I think that's the first time you've said that."

Once we leave the restaurant, Matt walks me to my dorm. I slide my key in the door and then turn to give him a quick kiss on the cheek. When he fully faces me, I kiss him on the lips.

"Sorry it took so long to reciprocate," I say.

A grin lights up his face. "Good night, Kelsey Faith." He gives me another quick peck on the lips.

"Night, Matthew Oliver."

Twenty

Since I was able to sit though service last Sunday, I decide to try service again. I'm running late and slide in just as the first notes of the second song begin. Matt reaches down and gives my hand a little squeeze. Luckily, this worship set contains new songs. I take a deep breath as we settle in for the sermon and try to listen. Apparently, this service is proving harder to sit through and I can't really place my finger on why.

Matt leans in close. "You need a minute?"

I glance over at him, and he bites his bottom lip, imitating me. I look back to the stage, not answering his question. Another few minutes pass and I excuse myself.

As people start to trickle out the doors, I head back to our seats. Matt stands with my purse and keys.

"Hey." He hands my belongings over.

"Thanks."

"Everything all right?"

I lift one shoulder. "Are you guys headed back to the dorms?"

"Lunch," Jake answers. "You're coming, right?"

"Um, sure."

Since the three of them rode to church together, Matt offers to ride with me over to the restaurant. The music fills the silence as we drive. Matt doesn't mention me walking out and I don't offer any explanation, mostly because I don't have one. It wasn't one particular thing that was said or done. The anger I've felt for months just crept back in and sitting in the seat just suddenly felt wrong.

I pull into the parking spot next to Heather. Matt stops me before I open my door.

"I know you don't want to talk about this morning…"

"It's not that," I say.

"You don't have to explain. You can talk to me when you're ready if you want to talk. Just don't let this one day stop you from coming back. It's a process, okay?"

I nod. He returns the nod and then we head inside.

I take Matt's advice and continue to show up on Sundays. It's hit-or-miss if I sit through a whole sermon.

When we reach April, I quickly learn April Fools' is very dangerous with Matt and Jake. I am the newbie, so I've fallen for quite a few pranks. The worst one—toothpaste in the Oreo. Heather has expertly dodged them all. Jake placed a fake ticket on her windshield, which she crumpled up and threw away. When we got back to the guys' dorm, Jake was eating straight out of a mayonnaise jar. Heather walked right over and scooped a nice fingerful and ate it. "I love vanilla pudding."

When Jake left the room, Heather jumped at her chance. She grabbed his phone, taking a screenshot of his home screen and moving all the icons to a different screen. She set the screenshot as his background and placed the phone back where it was. When Jake returned, she didn't say anything, didn't even look at his phone. I tried to act cool, but I was dying to say something. It helped when Matt walked in. I could focus on him. When Jake finally checked his phone, he grunted, fiddling with it for a minute before glaring at Heather and correcting it. I, for one, was quite impressed with her—also terrified. I knew I had to up my game next year. In fact, I had a feeling they went easy this year.

It seemed like the school year was quickly coming to an end. In just a couple days, it would be Easter, which meant a three-day weekend. Heather, Jake, and I talk about it over coffee one afternoon.

"So, what does your family do on Easter?" I ask Jake.

"An Easter egg hunt and lunch," he answers.

"I love going because his mom makes the best sugar cookies," Heather chimes in.

"They are pretty awesome," Jake says. "So, what do you do?"

"I usually do the whole church thing, and then I would go over to McKenzie's house for lunch." I pause, sucking in a breath. "But I don't know what I'm doing this year."

"Will Matt be joining you?" Heather asks.

"Babe, not really any of your business," Jake chides. She sticks her tongue out at him.

"I've thought about asking. I don't know if he'll want to."

"Why wouldn't he?" Heather cocks her head, sipping her coffee. The truth is, I haven't talked with him about it yet. I did mention inviting him over to meet my mom, who was on board, but the Fosters had invited me to their house as well. I considered going over as usual this year, but I didn't know how Matt would fit into the day. Plus, he had his own family.

I was still mulling it over later that evening when Matt and I went out for a date.

"You're being awfully quiet," he points out at dinner.

"Sorry."

"Something on your mind?"

"Just…thinking about Easter weekend."

"Are you ready to see your family?"

"Kind of." I pause. "So, what are your plans?"

"My family goes to church, and then we have a picnic lunch at the park. We are a big clan and don't really fit in anybody's house anymore." He pauses and takes a sip of his water. "I was going to ask if you wanted to join me."

"Oh." I chew on my lip, processing the invitation.

"We're a lot to take in, so I understand if you don't want to."

"I'll think about it." I smile at him.

He studies my face. "Is there something else?"

"No." I take a bite of food, trying not to let my indecision show.

"Kelsey, what's up?"

I sigh. "I'm just trying to figure out what I want to do. I've been invited to the Fosters' place, and I don't know if I want to go."

"Do you usually go over?"

"Yeah. John's parents fly in, and they always have Easter baskets for us. They claim we are never too old for Easter baskets. They're like family to me." I take a deep breath in. "But I think this year is going to be hard."

"I get that. I'm here if you need anything."

"I know. I also told my mom you would be close, so if your family is too crazy…you could come over to my house."

"Really?" He raises his eyebrows.

"If you want." I shrug, secretly hoping he'll want to.

"I'll think about it," he answers, winking at me.

After class on Wednesday Matt brings up Good Friday services at his church. "I know church has been a bit of a struggle and I understand if you're not ready. I just thought I'd let you know about it and let you decide."

Usually, during Good Friday services, the story of Jesus's crucifixion is read aloud and offers time for reflection. It's a very somber evening.

Matt continues rambling. "I know I didn't mention it earlier and it's not part of the weekend plans. I…well…"

I glance over at him, waiting for him to finish.

"I don't know what I thought."

"Can I let you know later?" Good Friday seems like a big step. I don't know if I'm ready, but I also know Matt will be there. I feel like, with Matt's support, I would be able to make it through service.

Matt nods.

Driving to my parents' house Thursday evening, I am still contemplating his offer. Since asking, Matt has not brought it up again, patiently letting me make my decision. By the time I pull into the driveway, I text Matt my answer.

Walking into the kitchen Friday evening, my mom stops stirring. "You're all dressed up. Where are you headed?"

"I'm headed out with Matt," I answer.

"And when do we get to meet this young man?"

I bite my lower lip. "He'll be over on Sunday." We settled on plans earlier in the week—I'd attend his family's Easter celebration on

Saturday, while he'd come with me to my parents' house on Sunday. I can't imagine how awkward the visit would be if he came with me to the Fosters' and I'm not sure he'd even want to go, so I resolve to go alone.

"Sunday will do. Have fun tonight." She smiles.

Matt picks me up early, but the parking lot is still packed when we arrive. There are even more people milling around the courtyard. Right before we reach the double doors to the sanctuary, I pull Matt aside.

"I don't know if I can do this." My voice comes out panicky and I feel my palms grow sweaty.

Matt takes both of my hands in his and faces me. "If this is too much, I understand. We don't have to stay."

I feel so torn. I tighten my grip on his hands. "Just…give me a minute."

Matt stands with me as we watch people trickle in. A gentleman comes by and closes the doors, meaning the service must be starting. I inhale a deep breath. "Let's go."

"Are you sure?" The little crease appears in his forehead.

"Not at all," I admit. Matt frowns. "If I have to walk out I will."

"All right," Matt concedes.

We enter the sanctuary, lights already dim. The chairs are arranged in a semi-circle. At the center is a large cross, lit in red. Below the cross are tables with what look to be communion elements laid out.

Matt leads us to two empty seats toward the back. I let him sit first and take the seat closest to the aisle. Strings begin to play and I turn toward the stage. Along with a small strings section, there is a guitarist, a grand piano, drums, and two vocalists. When the song ends, the lights go down and the stage seems to disappear. A video clip starts to play on the screen across the sanctuary. I assume from the backlight, there is a screen behind me for those on the opposite side.

The video depicts Jesus praying in the garden. When he walks back to his disciples, Roman soldiers appear, and Judas walks up to Jesus and gives him a kiss on the cheek.

I know the story—I've heard it a dozen times. The screens go dark and the pastor comes to the front of the stage. Behind him, I notice a black curtain and wonder if that's concealing the band. If I focus, I can make out shapes and see band members shift in their seats.

"That night in Gethsemane, Jesus prayed for another way. In fact, he repeatedly asked if there was any other way, let it be so. Jesus knew what was coming. He knew the pain and suffering he would endure, and he asked for things to be different. Yet, he ended each prayer with 'your will be done.'

"After Judas betrayed him, Jesus was beaten and mocked. He was made to carry a heavy cross up the mountain. He had nails driven into his wrists and his feet. Jesus suffered. Why? He could have easily chosen not to. He could have defied his Father to avoid the suffering that took place. I mean, he begged for another way. Any other way! So, why? Because he loved us. He loved us so much, he willingly died on the cross for us.

"When we think God could not possibly understand our suffering, think again. God gave up his only son for you and me. God understands. Jesus understands!"

I sit frozen in my seat. I feel Matt intertwine his fingers with mine and hold tight. A tear slides down my cheek, followed by another.

"Tonight, we remember the darkest day in history, where love suffered to save me and you. We are going to enter a time of worship. We invite you to come to the foot of the cross and grab the communion elements. Take some time at your seat to take them, on your own or with those you came with."

The band appears on stage and the low notes of the song begin. I hear the rustle of people moving.

"Do you want to go up there?" Matt whispers in my ear.

I shake my head.

"Do you want me to bring it back?"

I shake my head.

Matt sits a moment longer before heading up to the cross. I stare at my lap. No matter how many times I've heard the story, I don't think I considered how much Jesus suffered. I know I never thought about how much it broke God's heart to watch His only son die on the cross. Witnessing parents lose their only child brings that piece of the story to the forefront of my mind.

Jesus begged for things to be different. He knelt and agonized over this. When I think of the many times I knelt in that little chapel begging for God to save McKenzie, I never once imagined that it was God's will. I didn't want to think it was God's will that something so awful had to happen.

Matt slides in and takes his seat next to me again. A few seconds later I hear the little crunch of the cracker between his teeth and then the little pop of the seal for the juice. The band transitions into a new song and Matt stands to worship. I reach out and take his hand. He holds my hand tight but remains standing.

When the service ends, Matt gives me some time to compose myself before we head out to his truck.

It's quiet for the first half of the ride home. "Is that how you guys always do it?" I ask, breaking the silence. "With the band hidden and the cross in the center?"

"Actually, this was the first year for that. I thought it turned out nicely."

I nod in agreement.

"How did you feel about it?" Matt asks hesitantly.

"It was good." My voice cracks. I clear my throat. "Can I ask you a question?"

"Of course."

I try and gather my thoughts. Matt reaches over and rests his hand on my knee.

"Have you thought about Jesus's prayers? In the garden," I clarify.

Matt doesn't respond for a few moments. "Over the last few years, I've thought about the story, multiple times. I think it's hard to comprehend why Jesus didn't just say, 'Dude, I'm not doing this.' That's a very human reaction. We avoid pain at all costs. But Jesus wasn't like us."

"That's probably a good thing," I murmur.

Matt chuckles. "Probably."

Matt pulls up in front of my house. He walks around and opens my door. We lean against the hood, staring at my house.

"I wonder if Jesus felt like his prayers weren't being heard," I mumble.

"That's a fair question. Do you feel like that?"

"I think you have to be actively praying to feel like that." I pause. "But yes, I've felt like that."

Matt studies the ground for a moment. "I think it can seem like that, but 'your will be done,' right? I believe God hears *all* our prayers, but only acts according to His will."

"I'm not a huge fan."

Matt wraps his arms around me. "I know."

I lie in bed thinking about service and what good could possibly come out of losing my best friend. All trains of thought derail before I come up with a solid answer. I roll over and tap my phone to check the time—1:02 a.m. I sigh and close my eyes, willing my brain to quiet so I can rest.

Matt picks me up around noon on Saturday. As I'm pulling my seatbelt across, I catch Matt studying me.

"What?" I ask, glancing down at my outfit.

"Nothing. Ready?"

I nod and Matt pulls away from the curb. I take one more peek at my outfit, but I know it's not the outfit. He must have seen the bags under my eyes.

"I had trouble falling asleep last night," I admit.

Matt frowns. Once we are fully stopped at a light, he turns toward me. "Today is probably going to be crazy, so at any point if it's too much, you can just say so."

"I'll be fine." I give him a smile.

"I'm not joking, we are a lot. Sometimes it's too chaotic for me— and it's my family."

Driving into the park parking lot, Matt points to where his family is located. They occupy the largest ramada. Matt warned me, but I don't think I prepared myself for the true size of his family. My eyes widen.

"You sure you're ready?" Matt chuckles.

I give him my biggest smile, hoping I don't look too nervous. We walk toward the ramada, hand in hand. About halfway there, a little boy comes barreling toward us. Matt drops my hand and catches the little boy.

"Hey, little man." Matt tickles him and he shrieks with joy. Matt turns to me. "Dillion, this is Kelsey."

Dillion leans into Matt. "Hi," he says shyly.

"Nice to meet you," I say, giving a little wave as he clings to Matt's chest.

"Dillion is my cousin. He's…four now?"

"No, I'm five," Dillion corrects with a huff.

"Oh, right. You're getting so old." Matt sets him down when we reach his family.

"Hey, sweetie." A woman greets Matt and pulls him into a hug. He wraps her in a tight embrace before releasing her and turning toward me.

"Mom, this is Kelsey. Kelsey, this is my mom."

"You can call me Cindy," she says, extending her hand. "Nice to finally meet you."

"You too," I say, shaking her hand.

"Hey, are you helping with eggs?" a man asks, walking up to us.

"Oh, Jim. Let him be with his girlfriend this year," Cindy scolds.

"Where are my manners? I'm Jim, the dad."

"Kelsey."

"You can help too." He beams as if he's just had the idea of the year.

Cindy swats his arm. "She is our guest. We're not putting her to work."

Matt leans in to murmur in my ear. "Are you good here?"

"Yeah, you can go help if you want."

Matt and his dad grab a few grocery bags full of eggs and haul them to the large grassy area. Several of the kids notice and make an announcement. Suddenly, screaming kids flood the ramada. I find a spot to sit and watch as Matt and a few other grown-ups begin hiding the eggs.

"Crazy, huh?" Cindy says, sitting beside me. "I bet your family is much quieter."

I nod. "It looks fun, though. Easters were just McKenzie and I for the longest time. Then, Shelby came, and my aunt had kids."

"Shelby is your little sister?" Cindy asks. I nod.

One of the adults walks over to the ramada and gestures widely to gather everyone. Several of the kids race over.

"Shall we?" Cindy asks, rising. I stand and we huddle near the rest of the group. One of the adults barely finishes explaining the rules before the kids scatter like bumblebees in search of flowers. A little girl in a purple, frilly dress just sits in the grass admiring a pretty pink egg while her dad tries to coax her toward another egg. She is completely content with the only one she has.

"How goes it?" Matt asks, coming up behind me and wrapping his arms around my waist.

I lean into him, my elbow knocking into something solid. I glance down to see Matt's camera hanging at his side. "Get any good shots?" I ask, gesturing to the camera.

"A few."

I can't help but smile. Whenever McKenzie used to answer that way, I knew she had taken a few dozen, but only a handful would ultimately be acceptable. I wonder how many photos are stored on the memory card and which of those Matt believes are "good shots."

"I'm sure there are some treasures in there," I say and smile.

Easter Sunday arrives and I pick up Matt for church on Sunday morning, drying my clammy hands on my jeans. My parents have heard about Matt, but this will be their first time meeting him. When we reach the church, my parents are waiting outside. They must have already dropped Shelby off at children's church. My dad spots us first and introduces himself. Matt shakes his hand. My mom, never one to be shy, gives him a hug. We head into the sanctuary together.

The worship team begins the service with a fast-paced, celebratory song. Once the song ends, the pastor steps up and greets the congregation. "He is Risen! What great news. Turn to your neighbor as you're seated and say, 'He is Risen.'"

I turn to Matt.

"How you doing?" he asks.

"That's not what you're supposed to say." I wink.

Matt chuckles. "He is Risen," he says as we're seated. "Really, though?"

"I'm doing okay." I slip my hand into his and he gives it a gentle squeeze.

The church service is shorter than our regular Sunday services. Since Easter is a celebration of Jesus rising from the dead, the service is fun and uplifting. Afterward, we chat with my parents and then head out. I plan to drop Matt off at his parents' and then head to the Fosters' house for a quick visit. Just like we planned.

"Do you want me to come with you?" Matt asks as I back out of the parking space.

I stutter for a moment, caught off guard. "Y-you don't have to."

"I know I don't have to, but do you want me there?"

The noise of the engine fills the silence as I think about it. Part of me wants him there, but I don't want him to be uncomfortable. Like it or not, this is bound to be emotional.

"It's okay if the answer is no," he says gently.

"It's not that I don't want you there. It's just…there'll be a lot of people you don't know, and you've already met my parents today, and I…" I take a breath.

"Kels, don't worry about me. I'll go if you want me there."

I pause. "It would be nice if you were there," I admit.

"Okay. I'm all yours."

I glance over at him. "Really?"

"Yes, really."

"All right, then." I smile.

When I pull up to the Fosters' house, I spot a rental car in the driveway, most likely belonging to John's parents. I take a second to gather myself before getting out of the car. Once we reach the front door, I hesitate.

"I'm not ready for this. They could be just as bad or worse than my actual parents," I say, the words spilling out.

Matt places both hands on my shoulders. "Look at me," he orders. I gaze into his beautiful brown eyes. "It's fine. Just take a breath."

"Matt—" I start to argue. He takes a deep breath in and holds it until I follow suit; then, he lets it out. I do the same.

I turn back toward the front door. Usually, I just walk in. I remember John making fun of me the last time I stood out here, so I open the door and let myself in. Matt follows quietly.

"Hello!" I call out.

"Kelsey," Delia calls from the other room. She walks toward me with a beaming smile, wrapping me in a tight hug. "It's so good to see you," she says, releasing me.

"Hey, kiddo," John says, just on Delia's heels. "How are you?"

"I'm doing good," I say. My heart is beating a million miles a minute.

"So, who's this?" John asks, looking at Matt.

"This is my boyfriend, Matt."

"Boyfriend?" John eyes me suspiciously.

"It's very nice to meet you, Matt," Delia says, extending her hand.

"You too," Matt says, shaking her hand and then John's.

"So, how long have you two been together?" Delia glances between us.

"Just a couple of months," I say.

"How splendid." She claps her hands together, her eyes glittering as she inspects him up and down.

"I hope you're hungry. Delia made lasagna," John says.

I lift my nose to the air. "And garlic bread."

We laugh and they beckon us in toward the kitchen. I release a long-held breath, and Matt leans in to whisper in my ear.

"That wasn't so bad."

"You're incredible." I turn and smile at him. He handled those introductions with finesse.

"I know I am." He gives me a wink.

When we reach the kitchen, I stop suddenly, causing Matt to plow right into me.

"Jeez, Kels," Matt says, his hands landing on my hips. My feet are frozen. There, on the table, is my pink Easter basket, alone. Tears well in my eyes.

"Hello, my sweet Kelsey." John's mother hustles in from the backyard. To McKenzie and me, "Nana Foster" is what we affectionately call her.

"Hi, Nana Foster," I greet her, my voice cracking slightly.

"And who is this handsome young fellow?" She steps back to get a good look at Matt.

"This is Matt, my boyfriend," I say, trying to keep my voice even. I glance back at my basket. While Matt and Nana Foster exchange pleasantries, I peer in.

A package of pink Peeps sits on top, along with a few chocolate bunnies, some jelly beans, and other assorted chocolates. There is also a jewelry box. On big occasions, McKenzie's grandparents would get us something a little extravagant since they only came out a couple of times a year. Junior high graduation, we got beautiful sapphire rings. When we got our driver's licenses, it was a monogrammed keychain, sunglasses, and a wallet. I take a step back from the basket.

"Hey, are you all right?" John asks, stepping beside me.

"Yeah," I say. "Can you excuse me for a minute?" I turn and head for the stairs.

"Kels?" Matt sounds concerned.

I head straight to McKenzie's room. When I enter, I see the Fosters' luggage in the corner. Her bed is still in place, her dresser, her desk. But much of her stuff has moved. I notice some paint samples on the desk, and I can't rein in the tears. I sit on the bed, pulling my knees to my chest, and cry. The bed sags beside me as Nana Foster sits next to me. I know it's her by the smell—Baby Soft mixed with Tide and hairspray. I regain my composure and wipe my eyes. When I look up, the shimmer on her wrinkled cheeks tells me she has shed a few tears herself.

"You didn't have to do the basket for me," I say.

"Of course I did," she responds adamantly.

"I'm not your granddaughter, though."

"Kelsey Faith! You most certainly are. You have been a part of this family since McKenzie met you. You are just as much my granddaughter as she was. Do you know when my friends ask about my grandchildren, I always say my *two* girls are amazing?" She gets up and walks over to her purse. As she returns, she pulls out pictures from her wallet. One is of me and McKenzie sitting on the pier in Washington when we were visiting. The other one is from our high school graduation. "You are part of this family whether you like it or not. I expect an invitation to your college graduation, wedding, baby showers—all of it."

"Yes, ma'am." Leaning in, I pull her into a warm embrace.

"I love you, sweetheart." She wraps her arms around me.

When we wipe away our remaining tears and head downstairs, most everyone has retreated to the backyard. I step out to join them, but not before sneaking a few chocolates from my basket.

"I saw that," Delia scolds from the kitchen. I turn and wink at her. In the crisp air, Matt is listening intently to the story Papa Foster—George—is telling.

"She plops right down"—he pats the right cushion of the outdoor sofa—"and kicks her feet up." I realize what story Papa Foster is telling. John is snickering already, and Matt glances up at me.

"She starts to walk away when I notice she has something on the seat of her pants. McKenzie, who is sitting right where you are, also notices and gives me one of these." He proceeds to hold his pointer finger to his mouth. "Poor thing walks right into the house when Marie notices. The shriek that came from that kitchen! We were surprised the windows didn't need to be replaced. Kelsey comes back out, absolutely beet red. She's just yelling at McKenzie, 'It looks like I have poop on my pants. Why didn't you tell me?' McKenzie can't breathe by this point, and I may have chuckled a little."

"Really, the chocolate story?" I place my hands on my hips.

"Would you have rather I told the Easter Bunny story?" Papa Foster asks with a playful glint in his eye.

"It has to be less mortifying than this one," I say.

John is doubled over laughing at this point. "I'm not sure. They both have top billing."

Matt looks intrigued. I glance down at him and shake my head.

"I think one story is enough. Plus, I got back at McKenzie. I changed into her new pair of jeans, came right back out, and sat in the same chocolate spot."

"She about died right there," John says and then goes silent at the poor choice of words.

I swallow hard. "I thought she was going to leap across the coffee table and strangle me. She threatened if those pants were ruined, I was buying her a new pair. Luckily, Delia is a laundry wizard. She managed to get the chocolate out of both pairs, and by the time I went home, no one knew anything. But from then on, there was always a candy on that spot. Everyone knew to look for it, though, so whoever sat there got the candy." I look over at the empty spot and feel my smile fall.

"We always made sure it was securely wrapped, too, just in case someone missed it," John says and I nod.

"No one ever did, though." I chuckle.

"Dinner's ready," Delia calls. We all get up and head inside. As he passes, I give Papa Foster a big hug.

"So, this guy you brought with you. He a keeper?" he asks. I look ahead to Matt and smile.

"I think so. We'll see, though. That story may have changed his mind."

He laughs and gives me a mischievous grin. I shake my head, rolling my eyes.

After lunch, we say our goodbyes. I thank Nana Foster for the basket and give her a big hug.

"Next year, I'll tell ya the Easter Bunny story," Papa Foster promises Matt.

"No, you won't." I glare at Papa Foster, who shoots me a grin. "It's really not that good," I say to Matt.

"I look forward to hearing it," Matt says, completely ignoring me.

When we get to the car, I look over my hood at Matt. "Thank you."

"You're welcome," he says, his eyes saying so much more.

"I cannot imagine walking into a house full of strangers, having an emotional girlfriend, and remaining so calm, but you were."

"To be honest, I was a nervous wreck, and these aren't even your parents."

I pout.

"But they love you so much. They are family to you, and I am so honored you allowed me to come today. I loved every minute of it. Plus, that lasagna was freaking amazing."

"I know, right? Delia always cooks delicious food."

We head to my parents' house afterward. I walk in carrying my Easter basket.

"Welcome, Matt," my mom says as we walk into the living room. "You just missed the Easter egg hunt. The littles couldn't wait any longer."

"It's no big deal. Did they have fun?" I ask.

"I think we have to stop putting coins in the eggs." My mother shakes her head. "There was an argument over seventy-five cents."

"Oh no," I say, giggling.

"We have cake if you guys want any."

"I could go for some cake," I say and head into the kitchen, setting my basket on the counter. My mom follows and cuts a slice of cake.

"So, what goodies did you get this year?" She gestures with her head to the basket, sliding the slice of cake in front of me. She raises her eyebrows to Matt in a silent offer, but he declines.

"Candy and stuff." I glance at the basket. I snuck a few candies, but I never opened it.

"The Fosters spoil you." My mom smiles.

"Yes, they do."

"Kelsey!" Shelby exclaims, dashing down the hall toward me.

"Hey." I pull her into a hug.

"Is this the guy?" she asks, looking over at Matt.

"This is him," I say proudly. "Matt, I would like to introduce you to Shelby."

"Nice to meet you," Matt says, holding out his hand. "I've heard a lot about you."

Shelby glares at him. "Just so you know, if you hurt her, I will end you," she says in a menacing tone.

"Shelby!" my mom scolds.

Matt looks a little taken aback, and I burst out laughing. Shelby looks over at me with a cute smirk, and I hug her tight.

"Young lady, that is not how we talk to our guest. Where did you learn that?"

"McKenzie," Shelby and I say in unison. My mom looks completely lost.

"Tenzie taught it to me. She had me practice on Justin. It was fun. She said I could use it on your boyfriends too—make sure the guy knows who he's dealing with."

"You practiced on Justin?" I laugh. I wish I could have been there.

"Yeah. She told Justin if anything happened, he had to deal with two Lanter girls. Then she kissed him." She wrinkles her nose at the last part.

"You did good," I say, holding my hand up for a high five. She slaps my hand and then turns back to Matt, glaring at him with two fingers to her eyes to give him the "I'm watching you" sign.

"I see McKenzie covered all the basics," I comment, a hand on my hip.

Shelby smiles at me. "Yeah, I really miss her." Her eyes trail down, her smile vanishing.

"I miss her too," I say, kneeling to her height.

"I saved all my Milky Ways," Shelby whispers.

"Yeah? Those were her favorite. You always shared."

"Who do I share them with now?" she asks, her little lip trembling.

"I guess you can share with me or someone else."

"I don't want to, though. I want to share with Tenzie." A tear rolls down her cheek. My heart twinges.

I lean in as if I'm sharing a secret. "You know who else loves Milky Ways?" I ask. Shelby shakes her head. "Delia."

Her face brightens. "Really?"

"Yeah, really. I have to return my basket to her. We can put all the Milky Ways in and maybe make a little card. I think she would love it." I wipe the tears off her cheeks.

"Okay." Shelby perks up a little.

"Now, cake?"

Shelby nods vigorously.

Finally, after a long day, Matt and I have some time alone. We lounge on my back patio, eating Easter candy.

"I had a good day," I announce, unwrapping another mini Snickers.

"Me too. It was nice. A little scary when Shelby threatened me."

"Right? Who knew?"

"Makes me wonder how McKenzie would've delivered it."

"You would definitely be rethinking this." I wave my hand between us.

He chuckles. "She seems like she was an amazing friend. I'm kind of sad I never got to meet her."

Thankfully, Papa Foster's embarrassing stories and Shelby's threats didn't seem to scare Matt off. And strange as it feels, it was nice to reminisce about McKenzie. An ache still squeezed my heart, but for the first time, it wasn't unbearable.

Twenty-One

Unfortunately, the chocolate story did *not* stay between Matt and me. While Jake and Matt were hitting up the after-Easter sales and coming back with armfuls of candy bags, Matt made a comment about chocolate stains, which Jake caught. I told Jake it was nothing and gave Matt a hard glare. But Jake became relentless, and Matt finally cracked. Jake just about died laughing, but who wouldn't?

I begged them not to share the tale with anyone else. For a while, they were doing good, until Jake teased me with Heather in the room, causing Matt to chuckle. She knew she was missing out on something. I tried to tell the brief version, but the guys filled in all the details. Heather tried not to laugh but ultimately failed. I knew if I hadn't been the one in the jeans, I would have laughed too.

Only a few weeks of school remained, and the energy was palpable. Everyone was ready for summer—except me. To avoid thinking about it, I tried to keep busy with school and friends. The four of us are at dinner when Heather brings up their trip. The three of them had done an annual trip to California every summer for the past four years. Matt had mentioned the trip a few times. It sounded really fun, but they went over Memorial Day weekend. Matt told me I was welcome to come, but he completely understood if my answer was no. Heather, unfortunately, took my silence as a yes.

"So, what do you think?" she asks.

"What?" I blink at her, feeling lost.

"Going to the aquarium?"

"W-what aquarium?"

"While in California?"

"Oh." I study my plate, not answering.

"If you want to do something else, I'm open."

"Whatever." I shrug, pushing my pasta around my plate.

"If you're not a fan of the aquarium, there is always the zoo, or—"

"I don't really care," I snap, slamming my fork on the table. A couple seated at the next table glance in our direction.

Heather's smile falls, her shoulders slumping.

"Excuse me," I say, pushing away from the table and heading to the bathroom.

I know they are excited about the trip, and I appreciate Heather trying to make me feel included in the planning. I had told her I would think about it when she initially mentioned it, but the truth is, I haven't. In fact, I've been doing everything to avoid thinking about that weekend. I lean over the sink when the door squeaks open.

"Hey," she whispers.

"Hi," I say, resting my weight against the sink.

"Matt told me about Memorial Day."

I just nod, my throat dry.

"I'm so sorry, and I completely understand if you choose not to go. I would really love it if you came, though."

I'm about to protest when she holds up her hand.

"It's not just because I'll no longer be the only girl. I just think you and Matt are great together, and I have this feeling you'll be sticking around. I want you to be there. So many of our little inside jokes come from past vacations. I feel like if you're not there, you'll miss all the little things."

I look up, grinning despite myself. "All the little things, huh?"

"Yeah."

I walk over and embrace her.

She stiffens, stuttering for a moment. "I-I'm sorry. I have no idea what I said."

"I know."

Her brows remain furrowed when I pull away, and I don't offer any further explanation. I tell her I'll think about the trip, but I make no promises. In the meantime, they need to make their plans, and if I join in, I'll be content to do what they're doing.

After dinner, Matt and I take a walk around campus.

"So, about California," Matt starts. "I don't want you to feel pressured into going. I know it's going to be a tough weekend for you."

"I know. I don't feel pressured."

He casts me a doubtful look.

"Okay, I feel *some* pressure from Heather."

"Maybe we could change the date," he suggests.

I shake my head. "You're not changing it on my account."

"If you were interested in going, though, maybe it would be better."

"How long are you guys planning to be there?"

"That whole week. We found a great deal on a rental."

"What if I met you guys later?"

He stops, taking both of my hands in his. "Kelsey, you don't have to."

"I want to."

He looks at me skeptically.

"Look, you guys can drive out on the original date, and I can fly out and meet you. Then, I'll ride back with you."

"Are you sure?"

"If you can get me from the airport, then yes."

He nods slightly. "We'll work something out."

The week of finals has us all stressing out. One evening, I wander into the boys' dorm. Jake is on his bed, earbuds tucked in, a textbook in his lap. When he glances up, I give him a wave. He returns it before diving back into his studies. Matt is hunched over his laptop. I sneak up behind him and peek over his shoulder.

"Hey, that's me." On the screen, I'm sitting on a blanket smiling at the camera, the sun streaming through the pine trees behind me.

Matt jumps. "Jeez. When did you get here?"

"Just now. I knocked."

"I didn't hear anything."

"I know. You were focused." I pull Jake's desk chair over and take a seat. "What are you working on?"

"Final for photography editing class."

"Well, continue on."

I pull out my French book and my notebook, working through the vocab with the click-clack of Matt's keyboard as my study soundtrack. Eventually, I hear a few quick taps on the keys and then a huff. When I glance over, Matt is glaring at the screen. A giggle escapes my lips.

"McKenzie hated when photos wouldn't cooperate. She used to talk to them. 'Excuse me, is that what I asked you to do?'" I attempt my best impression of her. "It was hysterical."

Matt does not look amused.

"Except…when it's not. I mean, it's never funny when a photo is being stubborn." I try not to smile.

Matt's face softens, and he looks back at the photo. "She talked to the photos?"

"*All* the time. She was not a silent worker." I chuckle.

Matt sits back and watches me. It dawns on me then that I just referenced McKenzie…and laughed. I stare down at my lap, waiting for the tears to come or the pain to crush me, but nothing. Just a sweet memory of my best friend.

Matt reaches over and tucks my hair behind my ear. "You good?"

I look over at him, and I can tell from his expression that he's not worried. He knows I am. I give him a smile and nod.

Before we know it, the spring semester is over. It's tough moving back into my parents' house after living on my own for the past nine months, but I am just relieved I survived my first year of college. Over the next few weeks, I meet up with Matt for coffee or dinner. He even hangs out at my house on occasion. Shelby passes by us every now and then, giving him the "I'm watching you" motion. I stifle a giggle every time, though it reminds me of that gaping hole McKenzie left in my heart.

When Memorial Day weekend finally arrives, I drive to Heather's place to see them off.

"You sure you don't want to come with us now?" Heather pouts.

"Yeah. I'll see you in a couple of days."

"You're not gonna miss much. Just Heather being a major control freak," Jake comments, loading a duffel bag in the back seat. Heather smacks his arm.

"See what you're leaving me with?" Matt says, wrapping his arms around my waist.

I look up at him. "You'll be fine. You do this every year."

"Still." He makes a face.

"I'll be there in a few days," I assure him.

"Yes, you will."

Once they finish packing, Heather stands by the driver-side door, wiping the sweat from her brow. "Let's get going."

"Call me anytime." Matt hugs me, then leans in and gives me a gentle kiss. I sneak in one more before he climbs into the back seat.

They back out of the driveway and wave, and I wait for them to turn the corner before I head home. I swallow hard. I've been dreading this weekend. As everyone else is getting ready for camping trips and barbeques, here I am trying to hold myself together. It's almost been one year since McKenzie's accident. One year without my best friend.

I spend most of Saturday hanging out at home, receiving several updates and selfies from my trio of travelers. They look like they're having a great time. On Sunday, my parents go to church, and this time, I go with them. It's pleasant, even. Finally, the day arrives. I head over to the Fosters' house, letting myself in when I arrive.

"No, wait!" I hear Delia yell. All of a sudden, a little black and brown dachshund puppy is barreling toward me.

I kneel to pet it as Delia hustles toward me, holding a favorite pair of heels with teeth marks on the toe.

"Hi," she says with a breathy sigh.

I smile up at her, still petting the puppy. "Who's this?"

"This is Toby."

"Toby?" His little tail wags. "McKenzie always wanted a puppy named Toby."

"She did." She eyes him, shaking her head in mock scorn as she sets down her ruined heels. "We got him last month. It was pretty quiet around here."

"Regretting this decision?" I ask.

"No," she says, though her frazzled expression tells a different story.

"Honey, did you see this?" John yells as he stomps downstairs, holding one of his loafers.

"No shoe is safe, I see."

"This is the second—no, *third* pair this month." Delia holds up her heels.

John sighs, shaking his finger at the dog. "Come on in," he tells me, heading for the kitchen. Toby waddles behind him, tail wagging.

"So, how are things going?" Delia asks as we follow John and the pup.

I lift my shoulders, scrunching my face a little.

"You survived your first year of college," John points out.

"Yes, I did."

"Your mom tells me you're going to California," Delia says.

"I leave tomorrow night." I take a deep breath, my scalp tingling at the thought of the beach and the roaring Pacific.

"Is Matt going?" John asks.

"Yes." My cheeks grow hot.

"He was such a gentleman at Easter, and quite handsome." Delia winks at me.

I avert my gaze, still grinning. "He's amazing."

"I'm glad he makes you happy." Delia smiles, and John wrinkles his nose. I can't help but laugh at his expression. He made the same face when Justin entered the picture.

I spend the rest of the day at the Fosters' place, catching them up on my last few weeks of college and summer plans. We watch a movie in the evening, and I fall asleep on the couch. The next morning, I wake up to the smell of Delia's scrumptious coffee cake. Yesterday was rough, and I know the next few days will be just as brutal, but I can't let it stop me from living my life. My best friend wouldn't want me to.

The thought of her brings a pang to my chest. I miss McKenzie so much. I pull out my phone and access my voicemails, hitting the speaker button.

"*Hey, sexy!*" The voicemail begins just as John enters the kitchen. He stops dead in his tracks, and Delia freezes. The message continues, and we all listen.

"I just needed to hear her voice today," I say, my voice tight. Delia nods, tears rolling down her cheeks.

"I have a voicemail from her," John says, and both Delia and I look at him. "I listen to it from time to time. She had called that afternoon and asked me to send the recipe for cocoa cookies." He walks out of the room, returning with his phone in hand.

"*Hey Dad, thought it would be fun to make cocoa cookies tonight. Can you send me the recipe? Love you! Muah.*"

Delia chuckles. "She always ended voicemails with that. 'Muah.' Like she was giving us a little peck on the cheek. I miss that."

We spend the rest of the morning reminiscing. It feels good, almost therapeutic. I talk with Delia about those first few months, asking if she ever talked with anyone. She told me she and John saw a grief counselor for a brief time.

"Was it hard?" I ask.

"It was extremely difficult the first few times, but then it felt good to talk." Delia gives me a tentative look. "Why do you ask?"

"I went to a grief share group a few times. It was hard the first couple times, but it seems to be getting easier. I was just wondering."

"I'm so glad to hear you are talking." She gives me a warm smile.

After a nice afternoon with the Fosters and Toby, who has filled a full album on my phone, I head home. My mom drops me off at the airport late in the afternoon, and I try to calm my jitters, drying my sweaty palms on my jeans. This is my first time flying by myself. I text Matt when I board.

Can't wait to see you, he responds.

Once the plane lands, I haul my bag from the conveyor belt at baggage claim and walk to our meetup location. My heart starts to race when I don't see him, and I panic. I look around and check my phone. I'm about to call him when I spot Heather's car. Breathing a sigh of relief, I roll my bag over, tossing my suitcase on the back seat before climbing into the passenger seat.

"Hi, you." I smile at Matt in the driver's seat.

"What happened?" he asks, a little taken aback.

"You don't like it," I state.

"No—I-I mean, yes. It's different," he stammers.

"I know." I reach up and run my fingers through my new bob.

"It looks good, though," Matt says with that charming smile.

"Thanks."

"So, what brought this on?" he asks, pulling away from the curb.

"Well, Delia and I were talking yesterday, and I mentioned the plan McKenzie and I had to get haircuts before we started college. Kick off college life with a fresh new look, you know? She asked why I didn't do it now—start the summer off fresh. She thought it might be good and, well, here we are."

"Gotcha." He glances over, eyes roving over me.

"What?" I ask, a little self-conscious.

"Nothing. Just taking it in." He grins.

We stop by the rental house so I can drop off my stuff and change before heading down to the beach. Jake and Heather have set up camp. Towels, a beach umbrella, and a cooler occupy the space. Jake spots us first. "Yo, Kelsey. Diggin' the new look."

Heather looks up from her book. "Oh my goodness. You look adorable!"

"Thank you," I say to both of them.

Heather claps. "I'm so glad you're here. Now there's another girl."

"Hey, we're not that bad," Matt says defensively.

"No, but you're not a girl. It's different."

"Fair." Matt nods before dashing to join Jake in the waves. I take a seat next to Heather.

"So, how are you?" she asks.

"I'm okay, I think."

"I'm really glad you decided to join us."

"Me too," I say, and I mean it. I catch up with Heather for a while before joining the boys in the surf.

Jake eyes me first, and I hold my finger to my lips. He doesn't give Matt any indication I'm coming. I wait for a wave before pouncing on Matt, knocking him into the wave. Payback for pushing me into the pool a few months back. It totally backfires because Matt holds onto me, dragging me under with him. I come up spitting salt water.

"So close." Matt laughs.

"One of these days," I threaten.

The sun is setting when we head back to the house. Jake and Heather walk hand in hand in front of us, Heather laughing at something Jake said. I look down to see Matt's fingers intertwined with mine, and a smile forms on my lips. I don't know how to explain it, but I feel as though McKenzie sent Matt to me, or maybe she gave God her opinion. Matt was exactly who I needed. Our photography class was just an elective, but he really enjoyed it and now plans on pursuing photography, even looking at some art schools. His camera is attached to him at the hip. Apparently, I need a photographer in my life.

I still feel McKenzie's loss. It hurts that she'll never get to meet Jake and Heather, or this amazing man beside me. This man who showed me kindness and patience through one of the toughest years of my life. Who told me it was okay to be mad at God, but at the end of the day, to not shut him out. I started attending grief group and have met with Mrs. Carter a few times, which has been helpful. God and I still have a lot to work out, but I'm glad I haven't shut him out completely.

"You okay?" Matt asks.

"Yeah," I say, just as Jake trips on a slab of concrete. He stumbles but manages not to face-plant.

"Walking takes practice," Heather teases, snickering.

"Yeah, that's why she holds your hand. You'll get there, buddy," Matt comments, to which I burst out laughing. Jake drops Heather's hand and walks faster.

"I think he's getting the hang of it," Heather says loud enough for him to hear. Jake continues to ignore the three of us.

The little things, I think to myself. If I had decided to mope all week, I would be missing all of this. All the little things that make life fun, that make life memorable.

Acknowledgements

This book you're holding wouldn't be possible without a few people. First and foremost, my Creator. He let me know there was a plan and purpose for my life, and I wholeheartedly believe writing is part of that.

To my mom, for reading every variation of this story and giving me her thoughts and opinions and to my dad, who has been a quiet supporter of everything I do.

To my little brother, who will always be better at grammar than I am and has edited multiple scenes. He's also my go to person when I need an opinion on anything, including this cover.

To Carrie Ann, for reading scene after scene for all my writing assignments and polishing them up. So excited for you to read the full story.

To my little sister (from another mister), I count you as my first fan. You and Marc make beautiful babies and man that niece of mine!! The fox scene is all because of her. I cannot wait to see what gems come from my nephew.

To Brooke De Lira, for doing the initial edits and helping me feel more confident in the story I created. The story really started to come alive.

To Makenna Albert, who removed the fluff, rearranged scenes, and made sure any additions flowed nicely. This story sings because of you!

To Nicole Adair, for being willing to sit down and answer all my questions and give me publishing advice. I'm so grateful.

To everyone who read early versions of this story and provided critiques and feedback. Sometimes those critiques were hard to hear, but necessary.

To the team members at my neighborhood Starbucks, you keep me caffeinated so I can make it through my workday only to come back (yes, I show up multiple times a day) and write, edit, and work on cover designs. Basically, everything I needed to make this manuscript an actual book. It feels so good to walk in there and be greeted by name.

Finally, to you holding this book in your hand. I hope you enjoyed every bit of it. Thank you for making my dream a reality.

Karen Ramsey is an Arizona native. She comes home every night to her toy poodle, Pumpkin. When she's not crushing it at her day job, she's writing. Her blog can be found at caffeineandfaith.com. Since growing up in church she feels her life is powered by faith and caffeine keeps her going. She often wonders if there is a Starbucks Anonymous and should she attend, seeing as how when she walks into her neighborhood Starbucks she is greeted by name, no matter what time of day it is.